T0080982

ANIMAL INVESTIGATORS

KILLER SPIDERS

"That e-mail you got from your dad, what did it say, exactly?" asked the Prof.

"It said," began Max, "it said that he saw a monster spider, like from a horror movie."

"Yes, but it wasn't real," interrupted Meriel. "Ellis said so. Your dad was just seeing things."

The Prof went limping out of the kitchen. On his way down the hall, he checked in Ellis's bedroom.

"He's still not back," muttered the Prof anxiously. He had a very bad feeling about all this. Ellis had set out on his own mission to save Jack. But the Prof had a nasty hunch that both of them might need saving now. And from something much more deadly than imaginary monsters.

For more adventures from the

ANIMAL INVESTIGATORS

read:

RED EYE

GHOST DOGS

WOLF MAN

ANIMAL INVESTIGATORS

KILLER SPIDERS

S.P. GATES

USBORNE

For Laura, Alex
and Chris

This edition first published in the UK in 2009 by Usborne Publishing Ltd., Usborne House, 83–85 Saffron Hill, London EC1N 8RT, England. www.usborne.com

First published in 2008. Copyright © S.P. Gates, 2008

A CIP catalogue record for this book is available from the British Library.

First published in America in 2013 AE.

JFMA JJASOND/13   00081/1
PB ISBN 9780794533618   ALB ISBN 9781601303073
Printed in Dongguan, Guangdong, China.

CHAPTER ONE

Ellis Straker came walking through a drift of black smoke.

Suddenly he felt the ground shift beneath him. He yelled out a warning: "Keep back!"

Meriel, as usual, took no notice. She came right up to join him, glanced down at the crack that had opened beneath Ellis's feet.

"Wow, cool," she said.

Ellis could feel himself sweating as he looked down into the black abyss. At the bottom he could see red fire. He shuddered.

Like the gateway to hell, he thought. Then a second tremor came and the crack closed up, as if it had never been there.

Meriel and Ellis were on a mission. They were looking for an escaped alligator in the Wastelands. Ellis was a top tracker and Meriel could read animals' minds. Together they worked as a team, with their guardian, Professor Talltrees, solving animal mysteries.

"This is a creepy place," muttered Ellis, gazing around.

The Wastelands was a vast, unstable swamp, with creeks and quaking bogs. Dark trash mountains loomed in the distance. Fires smoldered beneath them all the time.

It looked like another planet. But in fact Ellis and Meriel weren't far from home. They could see the city where they lived from here. The Wastelands was right on the edge of it and had once been a huge garbage dump. But it had been filled up and closed years ago. Now it was just a poisoned, forgotten wilderness, wedged between the city and the river. Hardly anyone came here. Signs that warned *DANGER!* and *NO ENTRY* kept them out.

"We should have started earlier," Ellis grumbled.

He'd been waiting since breakfast to set out on this mission with Meriel. But she'd done one of her usual disappearing acts. She hadn't shown up until well after dark.

"So where were you?" asked Ellis.

Meriel shrugged, as if that was her own private business. "This mission's a waste of time anyway," she said. "Let's go home."

Home was the city's Natural History Museum – a massive, rambling Victorian building where they lived with Professor Talltrees.

"We might as well look, now we're here," said Ellis, kneeling down.

He was suddenly totally focused, like he always was when tracking, searching for signs in the mud that a gator had passed this way. It was almost midnight but he didn't need a flashlight. Light from the city behind them lit up the sky and cast a spooky glow over the Wastelands.

"That guy who said he saw that gator was stupid," said Meriel, in her most scornful voice. "Who was he anyway?"

"One of the guys who was building Mars Base One," said Ellis, his eyes still fixed on the swampy ground.

"Huh, Mars Base One!" Meriel spat out the name. She obviously didn't approve of the big glass bio-dome that had just been built in the heart of the Wastelands. You couldn't see it from here, it was hidden by a trash mountain. But Meriel shot a hostile look in its direction.

"Well, that builder guy was stupid," declared Meriel. "We should just give up now."

She glared at Ellis, as if daring him to disagree. Her gaze was fierce, unblinking – the kind wolves use to scare you. It would have freaked most people out.

But Ellis was used to Meriel's wild side, including her wolf stares. He *was* surprised, though, that she was giving up so soon.

"We've just started looking," he protested.

The gator had escaped from the city zoo three weeks ago. The zoo director assumed it was dead by now. But the builder guy swore he'd spotted it yesterday in the Wastelands. So Ellis and Meriel had been sent in to find out the truth.

"Your mission is simply to look for alligator signs," the Prof had told them. "If you see any, get out of there, fast. Leave the rest to the zoo people. They'll go in and catch it."

But it seemed Meriel didn't want to check for gator signs. She was agitated, pacing around. "I want to go home," she said.

Why's she so jittery? wondered Ellis.

The Wastelands was a dangerous place. But Ellis knew Meriel wasn't scared. She wasn't scared of anything much. And he'd thought she'd jump at the chance to get inside a gator's mind. Alligators have jaws that can crush bones. They can run like an Olympic runner. They can make vertical two-yard leaps out of rivers, to snatch prey from trees. They were just the kind of top predators Meriel liked.

"I told you, it's not here," fumed Meriel.

"Let's look a little longer," said Ellis.

"Ten more minutes," said Meriel, her eyes flashing. "Then I'm out of here. This is a joke! Besides, do you know how to track a gator?"

"I told you," said Ellis, patiently. "I've tracked crocs before." He'd done that in Africa, where he'd learned tracking. "A gator's not much different."

"*Huh!*" snorted Meriel, as if to say, *That's what people think.*

Apart from the Prof and Ellis, Meriel didn't have a very high opinion of people.

Ellis sighed. "Look, if I can't track it, maybe you can mind-read it, find out where it is."

"No point in trying to mind-read it," Meriel insisted. "Because it isn't here."

Ellis frowned. For some reason, Meriel was being a real pain in the neck on this mission. "I hate the Wastelands too," he told her. "It stinks. But I'm not going home until I've searched it."

He dragged a plastic bag off his face that had blown from the nearest trash mountain. The stench from the festering garbage and traffic fumes was overpowering. He turned around, letting the plastic bag fly off, like a giant white moth, into the night.

He didn't see Meriel's mysterious smile, or hear her murmur, "I *love* this place."

"What's that rustling noise?" asked Ellis. It was more than rustling, it was like the rushing of the ocean.

"Rats," announced Meriel, grinning. "Millions of them, moving around in the trash mountains. There are cockroaches, too, probably billions of them."

A long red cockroach scuttled over Ellis's foot, its feelers waving. "Ugh." He shuddered. "Maybe you're right. I can't believe that gator could be still alive. Not in this dump."

But the Prof had said gators can survive in polluted places. That this one could have swum through sewers to get here.

Ellis moved off, circling a trash mountain heaving with rats and roaches. From here you could see Mars Base One, rising like a huge silver bubble from the Wastelands. But Ellis didn't even glance at it. He was concentrating on the mission. And his sharp eyes had spotted something.

"Hey," he said, waving Meriel over. "Think I've found something."

Meriel crouched down beside him. There, in the mud, were some four-toed claw marks. They were on the banks of a creek. Little, twisty creeks, filled with water from the nearby river, threaded their way all through the Wastelands.

"It's a dog," declared Meriel. "A big dog. Bet

there's all kinds of stray dogs in the Wastelands."

"Could be," Ellis admitted. Gator prints looked like dog prints. What made them different were the sliding marks of a fat, scaly tail. And Ellis couldn't see any tail tracks.

"It's a dog," insisted Meriel. "Anyone can see that."

Ellis was used to Meriel being stubborn. But he was the tracker in the team. So how could she be so sure, when he wasn't? It was almost like she was trying to throw him off the scent.

"Well, I'm going to look some more," he told her. "You go home if you want to."

Meriel didn't start for home. But she didn't seem interested in searching for the gator either.

"So are you coming or what?" asked Ellis. While he was waiting for her to decide, he picked a golden spider off a grass stem.

It was tiny, small as a pinhead. He watched it, fascinated, as it ran over his hand and looped sticky threads between his fingers.

But Meriel stiffened. She was too proud to panic. Instead she clenched her fists tight, until the knuckles were as white as bone.

She hated spiders, even small ones like this. It was a primal instinct, deep in her animal nature. It was something about their eight legs, the way they rushed around. Even big creatures, like elephants, are scared of tiny scuttling things.

But, typical of Meriel, she'd never told anyone about her fear. Not even Ellis knew.

The tiny spider abseiled down from Ellis's hand on a long thread, then vanished into the grass.

Only then did Meriel relax.

Ellis said, "What's wrong with you tonight?" He was itching to be off on the gator hunt. He had an intuition there was something out there. The back of his neck was prickling. It was his tracker's sixth sense. You can be the most brilliant observer ever, see all the signs, but without that sixth sense you can never be a top tracker. Gift had it. Gift was the master tracker in Africa who taught Ellis his skills. Gift would say, "There's a leopard coming." And, ten minutes later, it'd stroll out of the long grass.

When Meriel didn't answer, Ellis dashed ahead, then disappeared behind some pale, ghostly reeds.

Meriel didn't follow. Instead, she waited until he was out of sight, then stood perfectly still. Her eyes took on a glazed look, as if she was in a trance. But her brain was active, searching urgently around, trying to pick up animal mind waves.

Maybe it won't work, thought Meriel. But she thought that every time. Her power to read animals' minds was unpredictable. Either it happened, or it didn't.

But this time it did. Suddenly she was locked on. And she wasn't Meriel anymore. She wasn't a rat either, sniffing garbage. She was something much, much bigger.

She wiggled further into the ooze to hide herself. Her belly was sunk in mud, but her eyes and snout were above the dark water. She stayed absolutely still. Her heartbeat was slowed way down, her cold blood barely moving in her veins.

A glittering firefly landed on her snout, before darting off.

Then high-pitched chirps sounded, like chicks in a nest. Suddenly she moved, clashing her great jaws, lashing her scaly tail. She hauled her heavy body up the bank, leaving sliding marks. She tunneled through pale reeds. Then she began digging like a dog, with her front claws, in a mound of mud. White leathery eggs appeared, the chirping grew louder, more shrill. Some eggs were already split and out of them wiggled black-and-yellow striped baby gators, glistening with slime. Another egg hatched, then another...

Meriel shook herself. The brightness came back to her eyes. She was back in her own body.

"You clever girl," she murmured. "You've got babies."

And there was something else surprising. It wasn't that animals had feelings. She knew better than anyone that they did. But while she was in that gator's mind, she'd felt something really unexpected. It was when her babies hatched.

"Love?" murmured Meriel, doubtfully.

No, it wasn't that. And anyhow, Meriel was deeply suspicious of that human word. But it was a fierce, a *really* fierce, protective instinct. Like the mother gator would rip apart anyone who threatened them...

"Ellis!" yelled Meriel. "Where are you?"

Then she heard Ellis call from the reeds. He sounded really excited. "I've found slide marks!" he said. "Come and look! There really *is* a gator."

"Get out of there!" Meriel yelled. "She's got babies!"

When he heard her, Ellis was squatting down, studying the tracks.

Babies? he thought, confused. Then he remembered – protecting their babies makes crocs super-aggressive. And gators behave the same way.

As he sprang up, he heard a hissing sound, and saw something streaking through the reeds toward him, like a heat-seeking missile.

"Ellis!" Meriel was shrieking as she struggled through the reeds to get to him. "She'll kill you!"

Even as Ellis's mind screamed, *Run!* he thought, *You can't outrun a gator.* Should he stand still? Or pretend to be dead?

But there was no time to decide. The gator exploded out of the reeds, her powerful tail launching her into the air like a rocket.

Ellis flung himself into the mud. As she shot over his head he caught a glimpse of the creamy white armor of her neck and belly. She somehow swiveled in mid-air and landed facing him. The gray scales of her back and spiny tail gleamed like metal. Her great crested tail thrashed back and forth.

Ellis lay very, very still. The alligator's small beady eyes watched him. She was an ancient beast. Her kind had been around long before humans, since the time of the dinosaurs. Her wide mouth with its snaggle teeth made it look as if she was grinning.

Ellis hardly dared breathe. He saw his own mud-caked hand stretched out in front of him. It was trembling.

The alligator growled at him, like a dog. For her, humans were easy prey. She could afford to take her time.

She thrashed her tail a little more. Then she lifted her body high up, on stubby legs.

Oh no, thought Ellis. He knew what that meant. She was going to attack.

When she'd gotten him, she'd drag him into the creek. If he was still struggling, she'd do a death roll to drown him. In Africa, Ellis had seen crocs kill deer that way.

He could already feel those bone-crunching teeth. Reason told him running was suicide – gators can gallop faster than horses. But panic drove him, stumbling, to his feet.

Then Meriel slid out of the shadows. She stood

between him and the gator.

Her hand flapped behind her back. "Stay down!" she whispered to Ellis without turning around.

"Are you crazy?" hissed Ellis as he sank back down into the mud.

But Meriel ignored him, as if, for her, only the alligator existed.

"Hello, Gator," she said. "How you doing?"

The alligator relaxed its body. Its great scaly head shook from side to side. It hissed gently at her, like a kettle.

Meriel stepped forward, a slight, skinny girl facing a killer reptile from Jurassic times. She was careful not to make any sudden movements. She put out her hand, very slowly, and patted the gator on the snout. It nuzzled at her hand, like a pet dog.

"Who's a pretty girl then?" said Meriel.

Ellis stared, astonished, petrified. *This can't be happening*, he thought.

From deep in the reeds came a sudden, shrill chirping.

"There's your babies," said Meriel to the gator. "Congratulations, by the way. Should call you Big Momma now."

Big Momma turned and lumbered off into the reeds. One last flick of her armored tail and she was gone.

"It's okay," said Meriel, turning around to face Ellis at last. "She won't be back. She knows we won't hurt her babies."

Ellis lay for a moment in the mud, his brain trying to work out what he'd just seen. Slowly, his fear gave way to anger. He staggered to his feet.

"You've been to the Wastelands before, haven't you?" he accused Meriel, his eyes blazing. He should have realized. It was just the kind of weird, spooky place that Meriel liked. The signs saying *NO ENTRY* wouldn't have stopped her. Meriel didn't obey rules – not human ones anyway.

"Sure." Meriel shrugged. "I've been here lots of times."

"And you've met that gator before, haven't you? You knew it was here! Bet that's where you were this morning, visiting your gator buddy!"

"Yeah, I was," said Meriel. "We're good friends. But I only met her three weeks ago, when she escaped from the zoo. Didn't know about the babies though. That was a big surprise."

"Wait a second!" protested Ellis, who thought Meriel was missing the point. "Why didn't you tell me about the gator?"

"Call her Big Momma," Meriel corrected him.

"Meriel!" said Ellis, exasperated. "Look, this isn't funny! Big Momma nearly killed me! You knew where to find her too, didn't you?"

Meriel nodded. "Course I did. She's got a den behind those reeds, in some tree roots."

"You should've told me!"

But Meriel didn't apologize. She never did. Instead she said, with her usual bluntness, "I didn't want you to find her."

"Why?"

"I don't want her to go back to the zoo." Meriel detested zoos. She thought they were animal prisons.

"She'll be better off there," said Ellis. "If the zoo doesn't catch her, they'll probably send a police marksman to shoot her. She's dangerous!"

"I don't want her locked up," said Meriel, with that fierce, defiant look in her eyes. "She's not better off in a zoo. She's better off dead."

"That's stupid," said Ellis. But Meriel's eyes were

flashing menacingly and he'd had enough drama for one night. "Let's go home," he said. "Ask the Prof what he thinks." Meriel might listen to him.

But Meriel burst out suddenly, "Please don't tell the Prof. Not just yet."

Ellis stared at her, surprised. Meriel had used the word "please." She didn't often bother being polite. And she'd asked him for a favor. Meriel usually wanted nothing from people. Animals gave her everything she needed.

But Ellis hated lying to the Prof. And, besides that, he had another objection. "What if Big Momma attacks someone?"

"She won't," said Meriel. "She won't go near people, not now she's got babies. It's just that we went looking for her and came so close to them..."

Ellis wasn't convinced. "We've got to tell the Prof."

"Not just yet," repeated Meriel.

Ellis frowned. Finally, he nodded his head slowly. "All right, not just yet. But soon. And think about it, Meriel, she'd be better off in a zoo."

Meriel glared at him. "No, she wouldn't!"

Then she turned her anger on Mars Base One, that massive bio-dome built of glass and steel. It shimmered silver in the light from the city towers.

"I hate that big glass blister!" she raved, shaking a small, bony fist at it.

The dome was the dream of one man – Jack Nelson. He was a famous explorer. He'd been to all the world's remotest places, lived with lost tribes, wolves and gorillas. Now he'd decided, "Mars will be my next big adventure." The dome would be his base, while he explored the red planet. He'd designed it personally.

"Calm down," Ellis told the furious Meriel. "It'll be gone soon."

The dome was only here in the Wastelands while Jack gave it a trial run, to test all its systems and equipment. Once he'd finished, it would be dismantled, taken by space shuttle to Mars and rebuilt.

But Meriel wasn't the patient type. She wanted the dome gone now, this second. "I hate that Jack Nelson," she fumed. "He's just a rich show-off. How dare he test his stupid dome here! Spoiling my Wastelands."

Ellis protested, "How can you spoil the Wastelands? It's already a dump!"

"Lots of animals live here," Meriel insisted. "Before, they got left alone. Nobody came here but me. Until they started building that place..."

"Well, I think it's great," Ellis disagreed. For months he'd followed the dome's progress on the TV news: watched helicopters dropping in building materials and then huge containers packed with animals and plants.

"It's like a mini world inside," said Ellis excitedly. "It's got a rainforest and a desert. It's got lots of wildlife, even its own ocean with a dolphin—"

"But why did he build it *here*?" interrupted Meriel, throwing the silver dome another hate-filled glance. "Why did he choose the Wastelands?"

"Because he says it's the perfect place to try it out. The Wastelands is a lot like the surface of Mars. It's even got some of the same toxic metals in the soil. And guess what?" said Ellis eagerly. "Did you know the Prof knows Jack Nelson? The Prof's taking me to meet him tomorrow. We get a personal tour of Mars Base One."

"Big deal!" snorted Meriel.

Ellis didn't tell her that the Prof hadn't been too enthused either. He'd only arranged the visit for Ellis's sake. "You're a scientist!" Ellis had said, surprised. "I thought you'd be interested."

"The dome isn't about science or conservation," the Prof had muttered. "It's just Jack's biggest ever publicity stunt."

Before he and Meriel left the Wastelands, Ellis turned and took one last look at Mars Base One, rising like a gleaming mirage from the polluted swamp. Whatever the Prof said, Ellis was really excited about their visit.

He thought, *I'm going inside the dome tomorrow! I'm meeting Jack Nelson!* He could hardly wait.

Back in the heart of the Wastelands, twenty-three black-and-yellow striped baby gators were hitching a ride in their mother's mouth. Big Momma held them there tenderly, as she swam down the creek. She was moving her family to another den.

CHAPTER TWO

Early the next day, Ellis was back in the Wastelands, with his guardian, Professor Talltrees. They were waiting for a boat to take them up the creeks to Mars Base One. Jack Nelson himself, the famous explorer and thrill-seeker, was going to show them around.

The Prof limped badly, which meant he couldn't walk to the dome. He'd injured his leg eleven years ago, rescuing Meriel from wild dogs. He had other injuries, too, from that time. He wore an eyepatch to cover his lost eye and had scars running down to his chin. He looked forbidding, even scary. But Ellis knew differently. There was no one, not even Meriel, whom Ellis trusted more than the Prof.

That's why he felt guilty for lying about that gator, for telling the Prof last night, "I'm not saying it's not there. Just that we never found it."

To take his mind off it, Ellis asked Prof. Talltrees, "So how do you know Jack Nelson?"

"I met him about ten, eleven years ago, in Africa, when he was living with gorillas. Your mom and dad knew him too," added the Prof.

"I don't remember him," said Ellis. "Did he come to our safari park?"

"If he did you were probably just a baby, too little to remember. He lived with gorillas for a few years, making TV programs about them. Then suddenly, he stopped doing that. Said it wasn't dangerous enough."

"That crazy guy," marveled Ellis. Jack Nelson was larger than life, a risk-taker, a real old-fashioned hero. "I suppose he is a show-off," added Ellis, remembering what Meriel said. "But you have to like him, don't you?"

The Prof didn't answer that question. Instead he said, "When I knew him in Africa, Jack had a partner – she filmed the gorillas. They had a baby son. I sometimes wonder what happened to him."

"Jack Nelson has a son?" said Ellis, amazed. "You're kidding me!"

"No, I'm not," the Prof insisted. "His name was Max. He'd be about your age now. I remember him toddling around in diapers with the gorilla babies. He played with them, slept in their nests. I think he thought he *was* a gorilla."

"Wow," said Ellis, "I didn't know any of this."

Jack Nelson had never, ever mentioned a family in TV interviews. He always said, "I'm a loner. I hate being tied down."

Ellis was eager to ask more questions about Max, Jack's mysterious son. But suddenly, he couldn't. Talking about Africa had triggered his own memories. Of the day, two years ago, when his parents were killed by poachers at the safari park where he'd been born and raised.

He shook his head, savagely, to scatter those

dreadful pictures in his head. A mosquito whined past his ear – the Wasteland had swarms of them. Ellis slapped it into a blood-red smudge on his neck.

"Here's our taxi service," said the Prof.

A little boat with an outboard motor came buzzing along the twisty creeks.

"Who's the guy driving?" asked Ellis.

The Prof shrugged. "Jack gave me his phone number. Apparently he's some old fisherman who grew up around here. He knows the Wastelands like the back of his hand, and he'll take people out to the dome – for ten bucks each."

"That's a rip-off!" said Ellis.

The Prof shrugged again. "Local people might as well make some money from Jack's big dream."

The boatman pulled up beside them. He had a hard, lean face and unfriendly eyes.

"Professor Talltrees?" he said, gruffly. "Climb aboard."

At first they traveled in silence. The boatman didn't seem the talkative type.

The Wastelands were different today. The chemical smells still stung your throat. Black smoke drifted around from the underground fires. But it wasn't creepy like last night. Early morning mist made it almost magical. Even the trash mountains, in swirling haze, looked like some distant, enchanted kingdom.

"Weird place," said the Prof.

Ellis didn't reply. He was looking nervously over his shoulder. They'd just passed close to the reeds where Meriel said Big Momma lived with her babies. Ellis checked for slide marks on the bank. Or any other sign of gator activity. But there was nothing there.

"There's a rumor there are caves under the Wastelands," said Prof. Talltrees.

Suddenly their silent boatman spoke up. "Where'd you hear that?" he asked, harshly.

"I work at the Natural History Museum," the Prof explained. "And there's a fossil there. Haven't seen it myself, it's in the stores somewhere. But the story goes that it came from those caves – that about fifty, sixty years ago, a boy brought it in, swore that's where he found it. They paid him for it. He said he'd go back down, get some more. But they never saw him again." The Prof shrugged. "Don't know if any of that story is true."

The boatman stopped the motor and let the boat drift. He stared at the Prof.

"Oh, it's true all right," he said.

"How d'you know that?" said the Prof, suddenly interested.

"Because that boy was my big brother, Evan. He told me about finding the fossil, said he'd sold it somewhere. He said, 'Keep it a secret!' But I wasn't going to tell no one. Besides, I didn't believe it. Evan was a big storyteller—"

"So how did Evan say he found the caves? There's no way into them now," the Prof interrupted.

"There was no way into them then," said the boatman. "Evan said he was eel fishing in the Wastelands and there was a tremor. He didn't take much notice because it happened a lot. But, this time, a big crack opened up right next to him."

"I've seen that happening," said Ellis. "This hole opened up right in front of me. It had a fire at the bottom."

"This hole didn't have no fire in it," said the boatman. "It led right down into the earth. So Evan wiggled in. He wanted to see where it went. That night he told me about it. He told me he'd crawled through a tunnel and found a fossil stuck in the wall. Said he almost broke his fingers digging it out. Then at the end of the tunnel he saw a cave. He reckoned there'd be loads more fossils in there. But he didn't go into the cave. Instead he turned back. Decided to go back the next day with Dad's hunting knife to dig them out. He was really happy. He thought he could sell them like he sold the first one. He told me, 'I'll be rich!'"

"So did he go back?"

"I don't know. He did take that knife though – it had a bone handle, I recall. Anyhow, we never saw Evan again. We searched the swamps for him. We thought he'd drowned. But maybe he didn't drown. Maybe he did go down to those caves, to dig out more of them fossils."

"But didn't you see the way down," asked Ellis, "when you went searching for him?"

"There wasn't no way down anymore," said the boatman. "If there was, it must've closed up. But like I said, back then I thought he was kidding me. But it seems I was wrong all these years. My big brother was telling the truth, wasn't he?"

"Well he obviously *did* sell the fossil to the museum," said the Prof. "He was telling the truth about that. But I don't know about the caves. You said he was a storyteller, didn't you? Maybe he made the caves up. Maybe he just found the fossil lying in a creek..."

"What's it a fossil of?" Ellis butted in.

"I'm not sure," said the Prof. "I think it might have been a crab. Which would make sense. We're not far from the sea here. And sea levels were much higher millions of years ago."

"Well, you find that fossil," said the old boatman. "You find that fossil and study it. Because after all these years I'd really like to know what happened to my big brother." Suddenly his flinty face seemed to crumble. "I still miss Evan," he said, in a choking voice. "He was as brave as they come. He was my hero, when I was a little kid."

Ellis looked away, embarrassed, as the old man wiped his eyes. He didn't know what to say.

But Prof. Talltrees came to the rescue. He dropped his cool scientific manner. His voice was full of sympathy for the old man. "I'll find the fossil," he promised him. "I'll study it and get back to you."

"Thank you," said the boatman, curtly, as if he wasn't used to saying thank you to anyone.

He started up the motor. "Always knew the Wastelands was an evil place," he muttered. "You know what the locals called it back then? They called it the land of lost dreams." The boat burst out of the narrow reedy creek. It zipped over a deep lagoon that looked like some kind of flooded crater. "Look under the boat," the boatman told them. "You'll see what I mean."

Ellis leaned over the side. For a second, it seemed his eyes were playing tricks.

Through the murky water he made out collapsed walls, broken columns and wide marble steps, all wavery and green in the lagoon depths. It was some kind of submerged building, or the ruins of one.

Then Ellis cried out, horrified, "There's people down there!"

He could dimly see two bodies, standing upright, waving their arms as if to say, *Help us!*

"It's okay," said the boatman. "They're only statues. Greek statues of ladies dancing."

Ellis stared down again. All the distorting ripples and reflections made it hard to make things out.

But he could see now they were made of stone. The two dancing ladies gazed upward, their staring eyes white and blank. Their long flowing stone robes had great chunks missing. One had half an arm broken off, the other a smashed face with no nose.

"That's so creepy," said Ellis, shivering. "I thought they were drowning."

The boatman said, "They freaked me out, too, first time I saw them."

The Prof was gazing down, fascinated. "Was it some kind of temple?"

The boatman laughed, bitterly. "It was a theater," he said. "Back in the last century, some rich guy thought he could build it here. Spent a fortune on a really grand building – his big dream! Those statues were on either side of the entrance. Or supposed to be. Anyway, the Wastelands swallowed it whole, before it was even finished. That Jack Nelson guy must be crazy. Doesn't he learn from history?"

They left the drowned theater behind, swerved into another weedy channel. The boatman sat hunched up, steering. He didn't speak again. Except when the Prof tried to pay him, he waved the bills away and said, "No charge. Just find out what happened to Evan."

He left Ellis and the Prof on a landing stage. A wooden walkway led over the swamp to Mars Base One.

They both watched the boat disappear into the mist.

The Prof shook his head. "I never knew about that submerged theater."

Ellis shuddered slightly. "Those statues are really spooky." Then he added, "But what about those caves? Think it's true there are caves under here? Think Evan really found them?"

The Prof gazed out over the Wastelands, rubbing at the scars on his face. "Who knows?" he said. "Strange places like this, anything's possible."

CHAPTER THREE

Jack Nelson was waiting to greet them outside his dome. "Professor Talltrees!" he cried cheerily. "Glad you're here!"

Jack was twenty years younger than the Prof. He was tall, wiry and tanned, with a red beard and piercing blue eyes. He fizzed with energy and enthusiasm. He was wearing his explorer's outfit of baggy shorts and khaki shirt. He wore it everywhere, even to meet the Queen.

Instinctively, Ellis glanced down at Jack's shoes. He always did that when he first met people, just in case he had to track them later. Jack Nelson was wearing hiking boots.

Jack strode forward and greeted the Prof with a firm handshake. He seemed genuinely pleased to see him. He turned to Ellis and fixed him with those keen blue eyes. "Hi," he said. "So you're Ellis, the famous tracker?" He shook his hand too.

Ellis blushed shyly and mumbled something.

"Bet your guardian didn't tell you this – like you, he's far too modest – but he saved my life once."

Ellis stared at the Prof and raised his eyebrows as if to say, *What? Tell me more!* But the Prof looked away.

Jack laughed. "Don't ask him for details. He'll only get embarrassed, won't you, Prof?" And he clapped the Prof on the back.

Jack's just like he is on TV, thought Ellis. He was mega rich and famous but not at all snooty. He was friends with everyone.

So why wasn't the Prof being friendly back? Instead of so stiff and standoffish? It was almost as if he didn't much like the great adventurer.

"I might need your tracking skills," said Jack to Ellis. "I can't find my dolphin. I don't know where he's gone."

Ellis thought it was some kind of joke. *Dolphin?* he thought. *How can you lose a dolphin inside a bio-dome?*

But Jack was dashing ahead like an eager puppy.

"Welcome to my little paradise!" he said. "I've got 2,000 kinds of plants, birds, insects and animals in here. Many are endangered species."

"Wow," said Ellis, impressed. Jack looked eagerly at the Prof, waiting for his comments. But the Prof stayed silent.

"Just wait until you see inside," said Jack, his blue eyes blazing. "The entrance is around the other side." He led them around the vast glass and steel dome. Ellis tried to peer in but the glass was too misty. All he could see behind it was a green blur.

"Condensation on the inside," explained Jack. "That's how I get fresh water. It's collected as it trickles off the glass. And of course, the trees and plants provide oxygen and food."

He rapped one of the huge glass panels. "Armored glass," he said. "Almost nothing can shatter it. If there are any aliens up there on Mars, they won't get in. And if they do, they'll have a fight on their hands. No alien takes over my space dome!" He laughed merrily, to show he knew little green men didn't really exist. Then he punched in the code and strode ahead of them through the airtight, steel door.

Ellis smiled too. Some people said Jack was Mr. Ego, an attention seeker. But Ellis couldn't help being charmed by the great adventurer. He was such a survivor, a risk-taker. He never had any self-doubt.

"Here it is," said Jack. "My big dream. The biggest adventure I've ever planned. I've sunk my fortune into it. I've brought over whole trees from the Brazilian rainforest."

Briefly it flashed through Ellis's mind how the boatman had described the Wastelands: *The land of lost dreams*. The theater had been some rich guy's big dream too, but now it was under water. The Wastelands had swallowed it up, in one gulp.

But Ellis shook off those chilling thoughts. He

couldn't believe that Jack would fail. Not here, right next to the city. He'd lived with gorillas, he'd fought grizzlies in Alaska. He'd had all sorts of amazing adventures. Exploring Mars was next on his list. How could the Wastelands defeat him?

An automatic glass door opened onto a lush, vivid green jungle.

"This is my rainforest," said Jack, stepping through.

Great trees towered above them in the clammy heat. They were festooned with vines and moss. You couldn't see their tops; they were lost in the gloom, high up in the roof of the dome.

"Most of the wildlife is up in the tree canopy," said Jack. "See that rope ladder? There are several of them. They take you up to the treetops."

"You've climbed all the way up there?" said Ellis, his eyes following the ladder up to dizzy heights until it disappeared into the canopy.

"Course." Jack shrugged, as if it was as easy as taking a walk in the park. "Lots of times."

The guy's a legend, thought Ellis, shaking his head in amazement.

A swallow-tailed butterfly, striped black and

yellow, flitted past Ellis's head. An orange tree frog plopped into a jungle pool.

There was a harsh squawk from up in the canopy. Ellis saw a red and green parrot swoop from tree to tree.

"So what does this trial run involve?" asked the Prof.

"Basically," said Jack, "it's to prove I can survive inside this dome. That it can provide all my needs – food, air, water – just like it'll have to do on Mars. So I'm shutting myself in here for a month. With no help at all from outside. And no film crew. Although I'll be making my own video diary, of course, to broadcast later."

"Think there'll be any problems?" asked Ellis.

"Naa," said Jack, shaking his head. "Maybe a few little glitches. Nothing I can't handle myself."

"Cool," said Ellis.

You couldn't help admiring Jack Nelson. With anyone else you might have thought, *What an arrogant jerk*. But Jack's childlike enthusiasm was catching. He made you think anything was possible.

But the Prof didn't seem to have fallen under Jack's spell. He was still expressing doubts.

"Are you aware how unstable the Wastelands is?" he asked Jack. "It's often shaken by tremors. I assume this dome's got strong foundations?"

"Course!" Jack assured the Prof. "We drilled down really deep, just like we'll have to do on Mars."

"I hope you were careful," said the Prof. "Some people say there are caves down there."

"Caves?" Jack shrugged breezily. "Why should they worry me?"

"Then what about air purity?" said the Prof. "That's always been a problem with space domes. Remember the scientists who tested the very first one? Bio-nauts they called themselves. The air quality inside their dome deteriorated – too much nitrous oxide, not enough oxygen. They were being slowly poisoned. They started to hallucinate and see huge spiders and giant pink killer rabbits."

Jack hooted with laughter. "Giant pink killer rabbits? You're joking! So what happened?"

"Someone opened the dome door, let fresh air in from outside. Once they'd breathed in some oxygen, I believe the bio-nauts soon recovered."

Ellis was becoming a little annoyed with the Prof.

He wished he'd stop bringing up boring, sciency objections, pouring cold water on Jack's dream. Ellis was totally entranced by Jack's dome. He thought it was a spectacular place. "Do you have any sharks in this dome?" he asked Jack Nelson eagerly. "Or leopards?"

"No way," said Jack. "No big predators, I'm afraid. I don't want my endangered species being eaten for lunch. Or me, for that matter! There's nothing harmful to humans here. This is my little paradise."

"Any gorillas then?" asked Ellis. "Didn't you live with them once?"

Jack nodded. "That was a long time ago. I'd like gorillas here – they're great guys! But there just isn't room. Besides, gorillas go berserk sometimes. Don't want them trashing my dome—"

The Prof interrupted. "Speaking of living with gorillas," he said, "how's your son, Max? The last time I saw him, he was swinging through the trees with his gorilla friends."

Jack looked a bit shamefaced. "I don't see Max that much," he admitted. "He lives with his mom now. When he's not at boarding school that is – St. Dominic's, here in the city."

"But he stays with you during school breaks, I suppose?" asked the Prof.

"No, not really," said Jack. "I'm away so much, you see."

The Prof frowned slightly. "So when did you last see him?" he asked.

Jack had to think about that. "It must be two years ago now," he said.

"Two years!" exclaimed the Prof, sounding shocked.

"Max and I talk on the phone though," Jack added hastily. "Actually, I must call him again sometime soon. It seems ages since we last talked. I've been so busy, you see, making preparations for Mars."

The Prof said nothing. But it was clear, from his disapproving look, that he didn't think much of that excuse.

Jack squirmed under that stern gaze. He couldn't look the Prof in the eye. "I'll tell you what," he said. "I'll call Max right now! Tell him you've been asking about him."

"Um, there's no cell coverage in the Wastelands," Ellis reminded him.

"Course there isn't!" said Jack, slapping his forehead. "What am I thinking?" He did a fast rethink. "I know!" he said. "Max is on e-mail at school. I'll send him a message later on the Mars Base One computer. So that's settled then!"

Then Jack changed the subject quickly, before the Prof could ask any more awkward questions about Max.

"Want to see how I make electricity?" he asked the Prof, eagerly. "Then I'll show you the garden where I grow food – I've got pineapples, bananas, corn. And you must see my air filtration system. You'll be impressed. There's no way *I'm* going to start seeing giant pink killer rabbits!"

Ellis was looking restless. Jack laughed. "You don't want to see the boring stuff, do you?"

"I'd rather see the ocean," Ellis admitted.

"Good idea!" said Jack. "You go there. Use your tracking skills. See if you can find that dolphin."

Ellis stared at him. "You've really lost it?"

Jack laughed again. "Not really. He's just a little dolphin. He's probably hiding in the coral somewhere. It's just that I didn't see him when I checked this morning."

"I'll find him for you," said Ellis, eagerly. "Where do I go?"

"That way to the beach," said Jack, pointing to a track that squeezed between the tall rainforest trees. "Just go exploring. We'll find you."

And Jack hustled the Prof off in the other direction.

Now he was alone, Ellis's tracker's brain took over. His senses were super-alert. There wasn't much wildlife down here. Like Jack said, it was all happening up in the canopy, where parrots flew and tiny squirrel monkeys screeched.

Then Ellis heard a rustling close to his ear. His head whipped around. A thin green snake looped down from a branch. Its tongue flickered in his face. Ellis reared back. Then he recalled what Jack Nelson had said: *There's nothing harmful to humans here*.

He laughed at his own fears. *This is paradise, remember?* he told himself. But he felt sweat trickling down his back. It was hot and sticky in the rainforest. He was anxious to get to the ocean. Did it have sea breezes? Anything was possible in this amazing place.

So Ellis plunged on through the forest.

A glass door suddenly slid open in front of him. Ellis went through it. It shut softly behind him.

"Wow," said Ellis, staring around.

In two steps, he'd gone from rainforest to ocean. It was just a little ocean, as big as a small boating lake – like a dollhouse, everything in the dome was in miniature. But if you didn't look at the soaring steel and glass wall that separated it from the rainforest, you'd really think you were on some tropical beach.

Ellis scooped up a handful of warm, white sand and let it run through his fingers.

The water was like green glass. You could see all the way to the bottom. In the shallows, crabs scurried around, and over by the coral reef, where the water was deepest, glittering fish darted back and forth.

Suddenly, he heard an engine whooshing. It was the wave machine starting up. The little ocean got choppy. Surf rolled up the sand and left a ribbon of foam.

This is magic! thought Ellis. *My own private beach!*

Once the waves had died down, Ellis looked for

Jack's dolphin. He walked around to the coral reef, peered into deeper water. Scarlet sea anemones waved at him. There were clefts and holes in the reef. Maybe the dolphin was hiding in one of them. But before he had time to investigate any further he heard the Prof calling him. "Ellis! Time to go!"

I haven't seen the desert yet, thought Ellis.

But Jack was a famous person, his time was precious. He'd done them a big favor, just freeing up one hour.

"Ellis!" yelled the Prof again.

As Ellis left, reluctantly, the machine started up again and perfect mini-waves *swooshed* onto the warm, white sand.

CHAPTER FOUR

Meriel was hovering in the sky above the Natural History Museum. She could feel the wind in her feathers. It was dusk, but her sharp eyes could see every detail. Far below, in the museum's garden, the grass stems quivered.

Meriel dived, went streaking down like an arrow. Her claws out, she was just about to snatch a mouse…

Then, suddenly, she was standing on a flat roof. The hawk she'd been mind-reading swooped away, with the mouse dangling from its beak.

Meriel scowled. The spell was broken. She was back in her human body.

She loved flying. That's why she mind-read birds so much. And why she came up here so often, to the roof of the Natural History Museum, where she could see hawks and buzzards wheeling overhead and know, if only for a few minutes, what it felt like to fly.

And the other reason she liked being high up, like lots of birds and animals, was that you could see danger coming. From this roof, she could see all over the city. She could see to the Wastelands, where Big Momma was still free with her babies, and where Jack Nelson had been living inside Mars Base One for seven days now.

From behind her, Meriel heard a slight noise. Was it Ellis? But Ellis hardly ever came up here. He knew this was Meriel's private place, where she came to be alone, away from people.

Very slowly, she turned around. And saw a bulky shape hunched in the shadows.

"Come out where I can see you," ordered Meriel.

The shape shambled forward.

It turned out to be a big, awkward pasty-faced boy. He was wearing a school uniform, with a green and gold school blazer that looked far too tight for him.

"How'd you get up here?" Meriel demanded. He couldn't have come up through the museum. All the doors were locked. It had been closed to the public since five o'clock.

The boy was staring at Meriel in wonderment. It was obvious he hadn't expected to find anyone up here. He came closer, his eyes fixed on her with a wide and innocent look, as if he'd never seen anything like her before.

"What are you staring at?" said Meriel, who had a stare herself that could chill your heart.

"Oh, pardon me," said the boy, with careful politeness. He blinked several times to make himself stop. His face settled into a dopey expression, his big clumsy head drooped, so that he didn't make eye contact. But he was still watching her, with quick sneaky glances, from under his lowered lids.

Meriel wasn't much interested in humans. But even she couldn't help noticing that this boy's feet were bare. And he had very grippy toes. Right before her eyes, they were curling and uncurling, picking up the gravel on the roof. The boy saw her watching them. He immediately stopped, self-consciously, and straightened his toes out. He stopped shambling too and stood up straight. That lasted about two seconds before he slumped again, into a lazy, arm-flopping slouch.

"Excuse me!" He straightened up again, muttering, as if he was telling himself off. But there went his toes, picking up gravel, putting it down as deftly as if they were fingers. It seemed he just couldn't stop them.

Despite herself, a little fizz of curiosity ran through Meriel. "How'd you get up here?" she demanded again.

The boy gave her another shy, sideways look. "Um...I came up the fire escape." His voice was a slow-talking drawl. He didn't seem startled now. In fact, he looked so dozy, he seemed about to fall asleep.

"There isn't a fire escape," said Meriel. "Well, there

is. But you have to lower it down from up here."

Suddenly, the boy's dozy face changed. His lips drew back, baring his teeth. He made a chittering sound, like an alarmed ape. "Whoops, pardon," he apologized, clamping his hand over his mouth. "Pardon me. I didn't mean to do that."

"That's all right." Meriel shrugged, noting that the knuckles on both his hands were thick and calloused. "You don't need to apologize."

The boy fixed her again with that bright, wondering stare. Then dropped his head again, embarrassed.

"I'm looking for Professor Talltrees," he mumbled. "Do you know him?"

"Yes," said Meriel, suspiciously. "He's my guardian. So what?"

"I'm Max Nelson," the boy told her. "Jack Nelson's son."

And, suddenly, it all made sense to Meriel. "Ellis told me about you," she said. "You're the kid who grew up with gorillas."

But she'd said the wrong thing. Max was already backing off into the shadows, as if he wanted to hide himself from her.

"It's no big deal." Meriel shrugged, in her usual blunt way. "I grew up with animals, same as you. Listen to this." And Meriel threw back her head and gave a long, eerie, heart-rending howl. People in the street below felt the hairs on the backs of their necks lift and threw scared glances up to the rooftops as they hurried by.

"I like doing that," announced Meriel, lifting her chin proudly.

There was a long, astonished pause from the shadows, as if Max was struggling to take in what he'd just heard.

Finally he spoke. "People don't like me doing gorilla things," he said, his voice sad and wistful.

"Then you're just not mixing with the right people," said Meriel.

There was silence again, as if Max, in his slow deliberate way, was digesting that information, storing it away.

But then his voice came again. And, this time, he was talking about why he was really there.

"My dad e-mailed me from Mars Base One. He's in trouble. I didn't know who to tell – my mom's overseas, filming somewhere. Then I remembered my dad said how Professor Talltrees saved his life once. So I thought maybe he'll help Dad again."

"So what kind of trouble is your dad in?" asked Meriel.

"He says there's a big spider in the dome, like from a horror movie…"

"A big *what*?" said Meriel.

Suddenly Meriel saw the glow of a luminous watch face. Max was checking the time. He made that alarmed chittering noise again. "Oh no! Got to get back. It's lights out at nine o'clock! I'm at boarding school," he explained. "St. Dominic's. It's over there." He waved his hand frantically over the rooftops.

The clouds parted over the moon. And Meriel briefly saw a large, dark shape drop to all fours and gallop forward, on its knuckles, right to the roof edge.

The gravel crunched. Meriel said, "Max?" But there was no answer.

Then sounds came echoing back. It was Max, making a polite request in an eerie, ear-splitting ape screech.

"Tell the Prof about Dad! Please, if you don't mind!"

The screech faded away. There was silence again.

Meriel rushed to the roof edge and looked down. There was no broken body down in the street. But she hadn't expected one.

She looked out over the lit-up city. The dozy boy had suddenly come alive. He was making a heart-stopping journey over roofs, leaping gaps, swinging from railings, his strong toes gripping ledges. Sometimes upright, sometimes on all fours, he never mistimed a move. He had perfect balance. And he had no fear, even though he'd seemed timid and shy before.

"Go, Max!" said Meriel, as Max flowed gracefully across the city skyline, using the skills he'd learned from his gorilla playmates. The sad, repressed boy was transformed into something beautiful and free.

She saw the gold on his school blazer glitter briefly, as he dangled one-armed from a parapet. Then she lost sight of him, as he dropped down to a lower roof.

CHAPTER FIVE

Meriel came crashing into Ellis's bedroom. "Know where the Prof is?" Travis, her pet weasel, was lying draped around her neck like a scarf.

"Wish you'd knock sometimes," said Ellis, without pausing his computer game. "The Prof's down in the lab, working on some woolly mammoth bones. What's up?"

"I've just seen Max Nelson up on the roof," said

Meriel. Travis rippled like a red ribbon down her arm and whisked out of the open window.

"Who?" said Ellis, turning around from the screen.

"Max Nelson, Jack Nelson's son," said Meriel. "But he's not a big show-off like his dad," she declared. "He's not like, 'Look at me! Look at me!' all the time. He's shy—"

"Did you say this Max kid was up on the *roof*?" interrupted Ellis. "What was he doing up there?"

But Meriel chose not to answer that. Instead she said, "Max said his dad is in big trouble inside Mars Base One."

"Jack's in trouble?" said Ellis, anxiously. "How does Max know that?"

"He says his dad sent him an e-mail."

"What kind of trouble?"

"Max said his dad saw a spider," said Meriel. She hated the way even saying the word made her shudder. Maybe if she could get inside a spider's mind it would be different. But she couldn't. Spiders' brains are too primitive to mind-read. They're not proper brains at all, just clumps of nerve cells.

"A spider?" said Ellis, relieved. "So what? Jack Nelson wouldn't be scared of a little spider."

"Max said this was a big one," said Meriel, her fists instinctively clenching at her sides. "Like from a horror movie."

Ellis started laughing. "What's this Max like? Is he weird or something?"

"No," answered Meriel. "He's not weird at all."

"Wait a minute..." said Ellis. A memory was twitching away inside his mind. And suddenly, in a flash of understanding, it all seemed to make perfect sense.

"Did Max say anything about giant pink killer rabbits?" he asked Meriel.

Meriel narrowed her eyes dangerously. "Are you making fun of me?"

"No, this is serious," Ellis assured her. "I've just remembered something. The Prof said, years ago, some bio-nauts started seeing weird creatures. Like massive spiders and giant pink killer rabbits. But the creatures didn't really exist. It was because bad air in their dome was poisoning their brains—"

"So you mean there isn't a big spider?" Meriel butted in.

"Naa," said Ellis. "Jack's hallucinating. Seeing monsters that aren't there."

"You sure?" asked Meriel.

"Come on!" said Ellis. "A big spider? Like from a horror movie? That's ridiculous. Jack's just imagining it."

Meriel relaxed, her fists unclenched. Out in the museum garden there was a shrill squeak, cut short. Travis had found a rat.

"So what are we supposed to do about it?" asked Meriel. "This bad air thing?"

Ellis made a quick decision. "I'll go out to the Wastelands," he said, "see what's happening."

"Don't you want me to come along?" asked Meriel.

Ellis shook his head. "It's okay. It won't be dangerous. I just need to open the doors – get some oxygen into that dome."

"Shall I tell the Prof then? Max said to tell the Prof."

Again Ellis shook his head. "Don't bother him now. He's busy. Tell him when he's finished working, if you like. But I'll probably be back by then."

Ellis wanted to handle this alone. For different

reasons, neither the Prof nor Meriel approved of Jack's dome. But Ellis wanted Mars Base One to succeed nearly as much as Jack did. With any luck, this little setback could be dealt with quickly, without spoiling Jack's big dream.

"I'd better get going," said Ellis.

He was tugging on his shoes when Meriel warned him, "Watch out for Big Momma. She's moved her babies to that lake – the one with statues under the water."

Ellis wasn't surprised Meriel knew about the statues. It seemed she regarded the Wastelands as her own backyard. She knew every inch of it.

But how did she know about Big Momma moving?

"You've been to see her again, haven't you?" Ellis challenged Meriel. "Since we went looking for her in the Wastelands?"

Meriel said nothing. She was very secretive about what she did when she wasn't at home. It was strictly her own affair.

"So don't tell me." Ellis shrugged. He grabbed his jacket and dashed out the door. "Bye, see you later."

After Ellis had left, Meriel couldn't get settled. She was a restless spirit at the best of times, but this was something different.

She thought about gorillas: those shy, gentle giants who spend their time chilling out, chomping on leaves, popping their fleas and scratching themselves. Except if you make them mad – then they go berserk.

She thought about Max, at his boarding school, St. Dominic's.

"Bet he hates it there," she decided. Unlike Max, or Ellis who went to the local City High, Meriel had never been to school. She was too wild to be cooped up inside a classroom.

It surprised her that she cared about Jack's son. She usually felt no interest in other kids. But she had something in common with Max Nelson. Like him, she understood the loneliness of not belonging, either with animals or with people, and the pain of not feeling comfortable in your human skin.

Back at St. Dominic's, Max Nelson lay in the dorm under his quilt. His body was rigid with apprehension. It was always after lights out when the bullying started.

He managed to fit in during the day – his teachers hardly noticed him. His school reports said things like *lazy* and *disappointing*. *Disappointing* because this was his dad's old school. And when Jack was here he'd brought glory to St. Dominic's. He'd been Head Boy and captain of every team. In the assembly hall there was a showcase stuffed with glittering sports trophies, all engraved with his name.

It was the other schoolboys who couldn't be fooled. They knew at once that Max was different. They mocked him until he couldn't stand it. It was then that his monkey manners came out – the grunts of fear, the screeches, the bared teeth – habits learned when he was a baby, that, no matter how hard he tried, came sneaking out whenever he was upset or scared.

And Max was extra upset tonight – about his dad and that alarming e-mail. Had he done the right thing asking Professor Talltrees for help? He hoped the girl on the roof would pass on the message and that Professor Talltrees would know what to do.

"Hey, King Kong, want a banana?" came a soft, jeering voice through the darkness.

A kid had offered him a banana once before, when he'd first started at St. Dominic's. Max had said, politely, "Thank you." He thought he'd made a friend. But then he'd gone and spoiled it all by peeling the banana with his feet. Max could use his toes almost as well as fingers. It wasn't at all surprising. Most children learn by copying other humans, but, from before he could crawl, Max had spent most of his time with gorillas. So, naturally, he copied them. He didn't even know it was wrong until he was sent, at seven years old, away from Africa and his gorilla friends, to boarding school.

"Ape boy, you awake?" came another voice.

"Bet he's munching on his head lice."

Max cringed under his quilt. They were talking about that other incident he'd never live down – when there'd been an outbreak of head lice at St. Dominic's. Without thinking, he'd plucked one from the hair of the boy ahead of him in the lunch line. Then he'd crunched it between his teeth. Gorilla friends do it all the time, when they groom each other.

Snickering echoed around the dorm. Then someone gibbered, "*Eee, eee, eee!*" making a sound they thought was ape-like – although Max could have told them it wasn't gorilla language at all. The gibbering spread from bed to bed until the whole dorm was doing it. Some were bouncing up and down, scratching their armpits, like monkeys do in cartoons.

Max clamped his hands over his ears. He tried to pretend his tormentors didn't exist and that he was somewhere else.

But where could he go? His mom was always overseas, making wildlife films. His dad, who was practically a stranger, was shut inside a dome for a month. Max hadn't seen him for two years. He hadn't had any phone calls or e-mails for ages. Apart from that sudden, disturbing e-mail about horror-movie spiders.

Of course, like everyone else, Max had seen his dad often on TV. People said he was a great hero. So Max was actually scared of getting to know his dad better. What if Jack found his son a big disappointment, like the teachers at school?

I've never done anything brave in my life, fretted Max.

It never occurred to him how much courage it took, coping day after day with the taunts and mockery of others.

Suddenly Max thought about that girl, the one with the not-quite-human eyes, who he'd met on the roof of the Natural History Museum. The one who'd howled like a wolf at the moon and said he was mixing with the wrong people.

Max got slowly out of bed. A banana was thrown at his head. It bounced off his skull. "I got the monkey boy!" someone crowed. Then, from the beds all around, came a hail of bananas, hitting him in the face. Someone switched on the dorm light; he was almost blinded. He turned this way and that, bewildered, like a gentle gorilla trapped by hunters.

He felt his lips draw back, not in fear this time, but in rage. He struggled to control it. Despite all the jeering and despite being much bigger and stronger than the other boys, not once at St. Dominic's had Max become aggressive. He'd learned from gorillas to be peaceable and slow to anger. Gorillas almost never fight. They know that if they do, they'll seriously hurt each other.

But tonight, Max was already upset. And now

he'd been driven too far. He could feel himself losing control. He tried desperately not to. He screamed a warning that meant, "Leave me alone!" But it just made them all hoot louder. Another banana hit him, right in the eye. That really hurt.

Suddenly Max's big body dropped into a slouch, his arms hung, his feet stamped a war dance. His lips peeled back again in a roar of rage. He leaped onto his bed and, with his head flung back, he howled a furious challenge. He beat his chest like a drum, with cupped hands – just like the big males in the gorilla troop who'd adopted him back in Africa, when his human parents were too busy to pay him any attention.

It was a spectacular threat display. Schoolboys cowered under their quilts. Others dived beneath their beds. Some just gazed, eyes wide with shock. Monkey boy had gone berserk.

School books were piled on Max's locker. He tore them apart with his teeth and hands, then pelted the bits wildly in all directions.

Then he sprang to the floor, turned three rapid somersaults and dropped onto his knuckles. He galloped toward the dorm window. With one wrench it came wide open. For an instant his toes gripped the sill and then, with a last despairing scream, Max hurled himself out into the dark.

For a few moments there was silence in the dorm.

Then came the pattering of bare feet and a gang of white-faced schoolboys in pajamas crowded around the window.

"Stupid monkey boy, he's killed himself, he's strawberry jam," said a boy, staring down into the darkness.

"Wow, he's never lost his temper before," said a second boy in an awed voice. Max was normally so meek, even when they mocked him. "We must have made him really mad!"

"We didn't mean it," said another, in floods of tears, "we were only joking. Is King Kong really dead?"

"We could get into big trouble for this," said a sharp-eyed, thin-faced boy. "When they ask us, we don't know what happened. Right? It wasn't our fault. We were all fast asleep."

CHAPTER SIX

Ellis was keeping a sharp lookout for Big Momma. He was about to pass the place where she'd attacked him. With all his senses alert, he scanned the mud for claw and tail tracks, listened for that sinister doglike growling.

When he didn't detect any signs, he relaxed, just a little. Meriel must be right. Big Momma had moved her family to the lagoon.

It had made him feel guilty, and also hurt his tracker's pride, to tell the Prof their mission had failed – that he hadn't found the gator. *I ought to tell the Prof the truth*, thought Ellis. *Big Momma should be back in the zoo.*

Then he imagined her, swimming with her striped babies among the marble columns and Greek statues of the drowned theater in that green rippling light.

Maybe I'll tell the Prof later, he thought.

Behind and above him, the lights of the city skyscrapers winked and car headlights flashed by on the highway flyovers. But down here in the shadowy Wastelands it was another world. That sea of pale ghostly reeds stretched down to the river estuary. The stinking trash mountains, swarming with rats, festered away.

Ellis followed a twisty creek between reeds toward Mars Base One. Supermarket carts and rusty old bike wheels stuck out of the mud. Gas bubbles plopped up from deep underground and burst with a rotten egg smell.

Ellis tried not to think what could be under his feet – layers of rotting garbage, slow-burning fires, even those caves that the boatman said his big brother Evan had found all those years ago.

But those caves might just be a tall story. The Prof hadn't forgotten his promise to the boatman. He'd searched in the museum storerooms for that crab fossil that might prove they really existed. But so far he hadn't been able to find it.

The thing Ellis was least worried about was that big spider. How could he be scared of something that was just imaginary?

Jack's probably seeing giant pink killer rabbits by now, thought Ellis. But a few whiffs of breathable air, even the smelly air of the Wastelands, should soon get Jack back to normal. *Prof said it worked really fast for those other bio-nauts,* Ellis reminded himself.

By now, Ellis had reached the landing stage where, just over a week ago, the boatman had left him and the Prof. He hurried along the wooden walkway. The great glass walls of the dome curved, misty and mysterious, into the night sky.

Getting into the dome took seconds. Ellis had an excellent memory – a good tracker needs one, so he can store clues in his mind and carry maps in his head. And, from his last visit, Ellis had remembered the code that Jack used to get into the dome.

Ellis punched in the numbers now. He pushed the steel door wide open to flush out the bad air.

He stood by the door and yelled, "Jack, where are you?"

But there was no answer from inside.

Have to go in and get him, Ellis decided.

He stepped in, leaving the steel door open behind him to let more Wasteland breezes blow through. He took a few experimental breaths. He felt okay, not even woozy. He wasn't seeing monsters yet – that must be a good sign.

He walked through the entrance lobby.

"Jack!" he yelled again. "It's me, Ellis! The dome's poisoning you! Come out here!"

Still no sign of Jack. The automatic glass door slid open, as if inviting him into the rainforest. Ellis hesitated. He was worried about the air quality. Should he go in or not?

If you want to find Jack, he told himself grimly. *You don't have much choice.*

So Ellis plunged into the tangled greenery. The door closed as soon as he'd stepped through. Ellis thought briefly about trying to wedge it open to let fresh air circulate. Then he reminded himself he couldn't. What if the rainforest creatures escaped into the Wastelands? They'd die out there – if the bad air hadn't killed them already. So he left it shut.

He hurried along the track, shouting, "Jack, where are you?" He still didn't feel like he was being poisoned – no hallucinations, nothing. Maybe the bad air didn't affect you immediately. Maybe you had to be in the dome a while before you felt its effects.

But, strangely, the hairs on the back of his neck were twitching – that tracker's sixth sense. He wiggled his shoulders to make them stop.

Above him, there was a single harsh screech.

Startled, Ellis jumped, and stumbled backward into something. He spun around, his heart clenching with panic.

But it was only one of Jack's rope ladders.

"Idiot," he told himself. He stared up into the canopy, a green blur high above him. Then he saw a brilliant blue and red flash as a bird swooped from treetop to treetop. It screeched again.

It's a parrot, he thought, all his tension released. *Get a grip, Ellis.*

He was pleased to see it still alive and squawking. *Looks like the wildlife is okay*, he thought. He didn't have time to check the other creatures though. His first job was to find Jack.

He'd reached the door to the mini-ocean. He went through. "Jack, you in here?" he yelled above the noise of the *whooshing* wave machine.

Then, suddenly, something slammed into his back and sent him flying. The next second, he was flat on his face in gritty sand, his arms pinned behind him. He struggled frantically to get up. He felt hot breath on his neck.

"Stay down!" babbled a feverish voice in his ear. "It's up there, in the roof."

Ellis twisted his head around. "Jack!" He broke Jack's grip and scrambled to his feet.

Ellis hardly recognized the great explorer. Jack's eyes were haunted, half-crazy, his hair wild as a caveman's.

In one hand he was grasping a length of metal pipe. "Come down here!" he shrieked, staring up into the girders, high above them. "I'll smash you to pieces! This is war!"

Ellis looked up too.

"There's nothing there," he told Jack, trying to keep his voice as calm as possible. "See, I'm looking up now and I can't see a thing. Just roof girders."

"You'll see it in a minute!" said Jack. "It's clever! It knows how to disguise itself!"

"Come outside," coaxed Ellis. "Where there's fresh air. You'll feel better then."

"No!" shrieked Jack, hysterically. "I'm not leaving this dome. It wants to take over. It wants my dome for itself!"

Suddenly he dropped the metal pipe. He slumped to the sand and huddled there, shivering and rocking himself back and forth.

It distressed Ellis to see the famous hero in such a pathetic state. "There's nothing to be scared of," he told him, crouching down beside him. "That spider doesn't exist."

"No, no, you're wrong," moaned Jack. "I saw it. It's as real as you and me."

"Look," said Ellis, deciding to play along. "Tell you what. We'll go outside for a minute. We'll make a plan together. Then we'll come back inside and get that spider!"

Jack stared at Ellis, his eyes scared but hopeful. "Do you promise?"

"Yes," said Ellis. "I promise. As long as you come outside."

Jack stumbled to his feet and Ellis led him by the hand, like a little child, back through the rainforest and out into the Wastelands.

Outside, Jack stared around him, at the trash mountains and sea of reeds, ghostly silver in the glow from the city lights. He seemed to have no idea where he was.

"Take deep breaths," said Ellis.

Obediently, Jack did as he was told, gulping in great lungfuls of air.

The Wastelands air smelled like rotting garbage and gasoline fumes. But Ellis could see it was doing the trick. Already Jack looked calmer, saner. His eyes were losing that fanatical gleam.

Jack put his hand to his head. "What happened to me?"

"You were hallucinating," said Ellis.

"I don't understand."

"You were hallucinating," repeated Ellis firmly. "You were being slowly poisoned by bad air."

"Bad air?" echoed Jack.

"It was affecting your brain. Making you see things that weren't there. Like that giant spider."

"You're telling me that spider wasn't real?" said Jack.

"No, there was nothing there," Ellis explained again, patiently.

Jack was dazed and blinking, like someone shaken awake from a bad dream. But at last he seemed to understand, and grasp what Ellis was telling him.

"You mean, there's something wrong with my air filtration system?"

Ellis nodded. "Lack of oxygen," he said. "It does strange things to your brain."

"The Prof warned me about that, didn't he?" said Jack. "I should have listened."

Ellis didn't comment. He thought it was more tactful to keep quiet.

Jack took a few more deep breaths. "Anyway, I feel much better now," he said. "At least I never got to the giant pink killer rabbit stage. Thanks to you, Ellis." He slapped Ellis on the back. "Action-man Ellis! You're a hero. You saved me from disaster!"

Ellis blushed and mumbled something. He knew Jack's praise was over-the-top, exaggerated, like everything else Jack did. But it still made him glow inside.

Second by second, he could see Jack's confidence come surging back. The great adventurer was recovering fast. His mind was focused again on his big dream. But it wasn't that monster spider that worried him now. He was thinking about damage limitation.

"Who knows about this?" he asked Ellis, anxiously.

Ellis knew what Jack was thinking. If the press found out they'd have a field day. Ellis could see the headlines now: *MARS BASE ONE POISONS BIO-NAUT! LOONY JACK SEES KILLER SPIDER!*

"The bad publicity will ruin me," Jack fretted. "I'll be a laughing stock."

"Only Meriel knows besides me," said Ellis. "And maybe the Prof by now. And Max of course. No one else."

"Max?" said Jack, puzzled. "Max who?"

"Max, your son," said Ellis.

"How does he fit into all this?"

"You sent him an e-mail, remember? At his school. Going on about a giant spider. That's how me and Meriel found out. Max came to us for help."

Jack shook his head. "I don't remember any e-mail. I lost it back there for a while – I really believed my dome had been invaded, by some kind of monster spider. I was ready to defend my dome to the death. But, I'm fine again now!" he crowed. "Those hallucinations have completely gone. But I need to fix my air filtration system, right away."

Suddenly, the ground under their feet trembled.

"*Whoa*," said Ellis, staggering. "Did you feel that?"

Back in the dome, something else had felt that tremor too. High up, in the roof space above the ocean, a thick furry leg slid out from behind a girder.

Outside, Ellis instinctively threw himself down and pressed an ear to the slimy Wastelands soil. A tracker can tell a lot from listening to ground vibrations. But Jack was already striding toward the steel door, impatient to get back into his dome. "It's nothing," he told Ellis.

"But..." began Ellis, scrambling up. He was going to say that it seemed stronger than the usual Wasteland tremors. From deep underground he'd heard an ominous rumbling, as if rocks were shifting, cracking open.

Jack, though, didn't think it was any big deal. "It happens a lot in the Wastelands," he said, unconcerned. He hustled Ellis back into the dome, with his arm around his shoulders. "I'll leave the door to the outside open to let some oxygen in," he said. "Just until I've sorted this air problem out."

"Won't the animals escape?" asked Ellis.

Jack shook his head. "No, the internal doors will keep them in. No creature in here is big enough to trip them. Except us humans, of course."

Leaving the lobby, they hurried down corridors, heading for the dome's computer room.

From behind the girder above the ocean, that furry leg still dangled down. Then seven more appeared. And a hairy body, in two segments.

It was a monster spider, a yard long.

Its eyes gleamed like pearls. They were milky, almost blind, from living in caves for so long. But its poor sight didn't stop it from being a superb hunter. Through its feet it could smell its prey and detect their slightest movements.

The giant arachnid abseiled down from the roof on a strong silken thread. It crouched on the sand, cleaning itself with its front legs. It cleaned its fangs, then the two feelers, called palps, on each side of its jaw. The palps had strange, lit-up tips that flashed on and off.

Then it ran, as fast as a velociraptor, from the beach into the rainforest. It was bigger than any of the dome's creatures. Big enough to trip the automatic glass doors. They slid open before it, as if in welcome. The small double claws, on the end of each leg, clicked as it scuttled through.

In the tree canopy, the parrots went crazy, squawking and flying away in terror. They'd quickly learned that that sinister clicking sound meant death.

The monster spider had climbed up from underground caves, through a crack caused by drilling the dome's foundations. It had been a tight squeeze, a perilous journey. But when it finally reached its new home, it had found spider heaven. It was the top predator by miles – the other creatures in the dome were easy prey. It had started with butterflies and parrots. Then gone on to bigger things.

High up, hidden in the roof above the ocean, was its last victim. It was Jack's dolphin, wrapped up like a package and glued to the girders. The spider had let down long, sticky threads, looped at the end, and fished for the dolphin. When it felt a tug on its line, it had rushed down, paralyzed its prey with one stab of its fangs, then hoisted it up to its lair.

It had been feasting on the creature for a week now. Injecting it with digestive juices that turned its internal organs to mush, then sucking them out.

But now the dolphin was just a shriveled shell. And the spider was hungry again. As another door slid open before it, its sensitive body hairs felt a breeze. Its feet smelled the reek of rotting garbage. Milky eyes glistening, it scurried out, through the entrance lobby and the open steel door into the Wastelands.

The dolphin-killing spider had left the dome. It had been the only giant spider, so far, to find its way up from the underground caves. But there was a whole colony of spiders under the Wastelands, hundreds of them. And that last tremor, the one that made Ellis stagger, had opened the narrow crack. Now it was a wide tunnel, a spider highway.

Already, other giant spiders were pouring through it, claws clicking, hairy legs rustling, palps and eyes glowing eerily in the dark.

It was only a short journey through the trash layers of the Wastelands into Jack Nelson's bio-dome. The tunnel ended in the desert, behind a cactus tree. Soon, the first spider poked out a leg.

The invasion of Mars Base One had begun.

CHAPTER SEVEN

In the dome's computer room, Ellis sat watching as Jack ran checks, trying to find out why his systems had failed so badly.

"That's weird," said Jack, after a while. "Everything seems to be in perfect working order. The air filtration system is fine. The oxygen levels are normal. I can't find anything wrong."

"Maybe the problem's fixed itself," Ellis suggested.

"Must have," said Jack. He grinned. "I mean, the only other explanation is that I wasn't hallucinating and that spider *was* real."

Ellis grinned back. "Oh yeah," he said. "Just like giant pink killer rabbits are real too."

As Jack and Ellis joked, the first spiders to arrive were already settling in. Some swarmed up into the roof girders above the desert, others scuttled through the sliding glass door into the rainforest.

They worked like lightning, using their spider silk to build webs and other traps for unwary prey. But the thread these monster spiders spun from their abdomens was nothing like the silk of normal spiders. Theirs was a thousand times stickier, stretchy as a bungee cord and strong enough to snare an elephant.

After they'd finished spinning, the spiders hid and waited...

A couple of hours later, in the computer room, Jack got up from his chair. He yawned and stretched.

"I give up," he told Ellis. "It's a mystery how the air got poisoned. But I've made sure it can't happen again." He checked his watch. "It's late, almost midnight," he said, surprised. "Time for you to go home. The Prof will be wondering where you are."

"About the Prof," said Ellis. "I was going to ask you something. Did he really save your life?"

Jack nodded. "It was in Africa. A cobra was just about to bite me and the Prof killed it with a hunting knife. Typical Prof – he told me off. He said it was my fault for getting too close. I tried to thank him. But he said, 'I don't deserve to be thanked. I've just killed a magnificent creature.'"

"Sounds like the Prof," said Ellis. "He's very hard on himself." Ellis hesitated. "There's one other thing I wanted to ask you…"

"Anything!" said Jack. "You saved this project. What if the press had found me babbling about giant spiders and waving that metal pipe around?"

"Well," said Ellis, "before I go, I wondered if I could see the desert? I missed it last time, when me and the Prof came for that tour."

"Of course!" said Jack. "You go ahead. First left through the rainforest, then left again. I'll catch up.

I've just got one or two things to do here first."

Ellis stumbled through the rainforest. It was gloomy, but not too dark to see. Outside, the city lights made the night sky blaze. And some of that brightness found its way through the misty glass.

Ellis suddenly felt very weary. Like Jack, he hadn't realized how late it was – you lost all sense of time in the dome. But he felt happy too. His mission had been a big success. Jack had completely recovered from the bad-air incident. He was back in control of Mars Base One. And no one ever needed to know that his project had come so close to meltdown.

Ellis took first left in the rainforest. He gazed up into the shadowy treetops. It was strange how silent it was up there. Why weren't the parrots squawking, the tiny squirrel monkeys chittering? Maybe they were asleep.

Then he heard a strange clicking sound that he couldn't identify. *Some* animal was awake up there.

"There are lights!" Ellis marveled. Little twinkling lights like stars. Two flashed on and off. Then two sparkled in another tree, as if answering. Something was going on up there. But he couldn't figure out what.

I should climb up a rope ladder, thought Ellis. *Investigate.*

But he was just too tired. Climbing one of those ladders seemed crazy, when he could barely put one foot in front of the other. He even wondered why he didn't go home, leave the desert until another day.

But he was already there. He could see sand, thorny scrub and cactus trees through a glass wall.

"Might as well have a quick look," Ellis told himself.

The glass door slid open. A blast of hot, dry air hit him. He didn't notice two long sticky threads, with looped ends, that came slithering down behind him from the rainforest treetops. As he stepped through the door into the desert, they missed his head by inches.

Ellis was off his guard when he went into the dunes. Tiredness dulled his brain. And the dome had lulled him into a false sense of security. You don't expect danger in paradise.

His tracker's sixth sense tried again to warn him. The back of his neck was itching like crazy. But Ellis just gave another great, sleepy yawn and wiggled his shoulders to stop it.

If he'd been more awake, he would have spotted the tunnel entrance, even though the spiders had disguised it with a hinged trapdoor, made of sand mixed with fast-drying silk that had already set like cement. But, drowsily, Ellis walked straight over it.

The trapdoor rose, very quietly, just a few inches. From beneath it, pearly eyes glittered. But they couldn't see their victim. The clawed tips of eight legs poked out like a bunch of giant hairy bananas. Each tip touched one of eight trip lines that fanned out from the tunnel entrance. Those leg-tips could feel the tiniest tug. The feet could smell food nearby. The spider clicked its claws with excitement. It waved its glowing palps to alert others, further back down the tunnel. Then it stayed absolutely still, waiting to ambush whatever moved.

Ellis heard a voice from the rainforest: "Where are you?" It was Jack coming to look for him. At the same time Ellis saw the tripwire, a thin silken thread, sneakily stretched across the desert sand.

At last, his tracker's senses kicked in. *It's a trap!* Ellis realized.

But it was too late. His shoe had brushed it. It was the gentlest touch, but the spider had felt it.

Then everything happened with terrible swiftness. Sticky threads looped around his ankles and tightened. With one tug, Ellis was yanked off his feet. He felt himself being dragged across the sand. His hands clawed at it, leaving long five-fingered trails. Jack appeared, horrified, in the doorway. For a few seconds he seemed frozen with shock.

"Help me!" yelled Ellis, his eyes wide with panic, his hands scrabbling.

Desperately, he grabbed hold of a cactus, crying out as the spines pierced his skin. But he couldn't hold on. His hands were ripped from the cactus, and he was hauled feet-first down the hole. He saw the trapdoor drop back into place above him and he was in darkness.

He panicked, struggling and shouting. Small cramped spaces had always been his worst nightmare. But then came a much greater terror. There was a sinister rustling – a furry leg brushed his cheek.

There's something alive in here! his brain screamed at him.

Then Ellis completely lost it, yelling out in the dark among shuffling legs, grotesque hairy bodies, half-blind milky eyes.

He was totally helpless. He was flipped over and over, bound up by busy legs, Egyptian-mummy style. There was a stab of hot pain in his thigh. He cried out, once, but then paralysis struck all his muscles and his vocal cords and he was fighting for breath. He felt himself sliding into blackness. Then he passed out.

Up in the desert, Jack had sprung into action. He tore frantically at the trapdoor, trying to pry it open. He could hear Ellis just beneath it, screaming for help.

"I'm coming, Ellis. I'm coming!" Jack was shouting, not noticing that Ellis had suddenly gone quiet.

The trapdoor was a tight fit. Finally Jack wrenched it open and peered into the hole. All he saw was an empty tunnel.

CHAPTER EIGHT

Meanwhile, back at the Natural History Museum, the Prof had finally come up from his lab.

He looked at his watch and yawned. "It's after midnight!" He'd lost track of time, working on the thigh bone of a woolly mammoth found frozen in the Russian tundra.

Meriel was pacing around the kitchen, like a caged animal in a zoo.

"Hello, Meriel," said the Prof. He was surprised to see her. He'd expected her to be on one of her nighttime wanderings.

"Ellis isn't back yet," Meriel blurted out.

Meriel liked to think that she didn't care much about people. That they weren't as important to her as animals. But sometimes her human heart told her differently. As the night wore on and Ellis didn't return, she'd become increasingly worried about him. "He said he'd be back!" she told the Prof, angrily, as if she hated her own anxiety.

"Why, where is Ellis?" asked the Prof, a tiny twist of unease wiggling inside him.

"He should be back!" said Meriel, stomping around.

"What's going on?" the Prof asked his ward gently. "Just tell me."

Meriel whirled around to face him. Suddenly, words poured out of her mouth – about Max Nelson and a giant spider and Ellis.

"Stop a minute," said the Prof. "Did you say spider?"

Meriel writhed and twisted, like Travis her weasel. She didn't want to dwell on that giant spider. Even though Ellis had assured her it didn't exist, just talking about it spooked her.

The Prof had no idea about her spider phobia. He just knew you had to be patient with Meriel. It was no use trying to force her to do anything. Gradually, he managed to coax the whole story out of her. How Ellis was sure that somehow the dome's air had gotten poisoned, and how he thought Jack was only hallucinating.

After she'd finished, the Prof frowned.

"I can't understand all this," he told her. "It doesn't make any sense. Jack showed me his air filtration system. It was impossible for it to fail. There were alarm systems, all sorts of safeguards."

"But Ellis said that spider wasn't real," scowled Meriel, clenching her small, bony fists into knots. "So his air filtration system must be to blame."

The Prof rubbed at the scar on his face. "I just wish Ellis had consulted me before he went."

"I'm going out now," declared Meriel, with sudden urgency. She was still worried about Ellis. But images of scuttling spiders had invaded her mind. And she just couldn't cope with it.

The Prof hardly noticed as his ward went

whisking out of the kitchen. He was deep in thought.

Meriel climbed up to the flat roof of the Natural History Museum, her usual refuge when she couldn't handle emotions that overwhelmed her – when she needed some space and freedom.

Maybe there'd be an owl she could mind-read. Flying like a bird – for Meriel that was the best escape of all.

She stood there for a long time, breathing in the cool night air, gazing up at the starry, inky-blue sky. Slowly, the spiders in her head crept away.

Suddenly there was a chilling, unearthly shriek. Something swooped silently, like a silver ghost, from dark tree to dark tree down in the museum gardens. It was an owl, out hunting. Meriel smiled.

She was halfway into her trance, feeling her mind slipping from her body, when she was jerked back to the rooftop by a noise in her ear. It was a mournful, hooting sound.

That's not an owl, thought Meriel, immediately.

She whirled around. And there was Max, shambling up to her in his striped pajamas.

"I've run away from school," he told her, with

more sad hoots of distress. "And I'm never going back."

Meriel didn't express any surprise, or say, "You'll be in big trouble!" She just said, "You better come down to the kitchen and meet Professor Talltrees."

"This is Max Nelson," said Meriel unceremoniously.

The Prof was still sitting at the kitchen table, thinking deeply. He looked around, distracted. "Who?"

"Max Nelson," repeated Meriel. "The son of that Jack Nelson guy."

The Prof leaped up. "Max!" he said, surprised. He strode toward Max and shook his hand, greeted him like a long-lost friend. "It's good to see you again. You won't remember me but I knew your dad, in Africa. Sit down, sit down! Would you like something to drink?"

He pushed a can of Coke toward Max.

Max took it, dumbly, startled for a moment by that pirate's eyepatch, that forbidding, scarred face.

But the Prof seemed kind. And not at all put off by Max's strange facial expressions or the gorilla sounds that always escaped from his mouth when he was upset. Suddenly, Max found his voice.

"I'm never, ever going back to school," he told the Prof vehemently, gripping the can so hard in his strong fingers that it started crumpling.

"Okay," said the Prof, calmly. "We can talk about that later. But what I want to know now is – that e-mail you got from your dad, what did it say, exactly?"

"It said," began Max, in that slow, deliberate voice that fooled people into thinking he wasn't very bright, "it said that he saw a monster spider, like from a horror movie."

"Yes, but it wasn't real," interrupted Meriel. "Ellis said so. Your dad was just seeing things."

Max swung his big head toward Meriel, his eyes wide in that wondering stare. "Does that mean my dad's not in any danger?"

"Naa," said Meriel, dismissively. She explained briefly about the poisoned air. Then she said, "Don't worry. Ellis will sort everything out."

Max looked puzzled, relieved and grateful all at the same time. "Pardon me, but who *is* Ellis?" he asked.

Before Meriel could reply, the Prof tapped Max's shoulder, to get his attention back. "Did the e-mail say anything else?" he asked, his voice more insistent.

"Most of it didn't make sense," said Max. "Like my dad was crazy or something. But it said about the claws."

"What claws?" asked the Prof, leaning urgently forward.

"It said the spider had claws, two claws, on the end of each leg," said Max. "And I thought, that's weird, 'cos I didn't know spiders had claws. But that doesn't matter now, does it?" Max appealed to the Prof. "Because, if my dad just imagined that spider anyway..."

"He did imagine it, I just told you," Meriel burst out angrily, springing up from her seat. "So let's just stop talking about stupid spiders!"

But for once, the Prof ignored her. He pointed a stern finger at Max and Meriel. "Stay here, you two," he ordered. "Don't go wandering off. I'm going to find something."

He went limping out of the kitchen. On his way down the hall, he checked in Ellis's bedroom.

"He's still not back," muttered the Prof anxiously. He had a very bad feeling about all this. Ellis had set out on his own mission to save Jack. But the Prof had a nasty hunch that both of them might need saving now. And from something much more deadly than imaginary monsters.

"I just hope I'm wrong, that's all," murmured the Prof to himself. He hurried, as fast as his lame leg would let him, down to the museum storerooms in the basement.

"What's he so worked up about?" wondered Meriel, staring after her guardian.

For some minutes she seemed to have forgotten Max. She was pacing around, her hands still clenched into fists at her sides, muttering, "It's not real. It's not real."

Max watched her, his head swinging back and forth as she stormed up and down. Meriel hadn't met many other children. And, when she did, some of them found her creepy. She scared them. That fierce, feral look in her eyes, the way she seemed to size them up as prey, made them run for their mothers. At the very least, kids found her haughty and unfriendly.

But Max wasn't put off. Instead his innocent gorilla gaze became even more marveling and wide-eyed. He seemed to know instinctively that, for the first time in his whole life, he'd found a human being he could connect with.

"When you howled like that..." Max began hesitantly.

Meriel was still angry with herself for letting all that talk of spiders make her shudder. She glared at Max.

"It's 'cos I lived with wild dogs," she snapped. "They taught me to do that."

Max wasn't put off by her aggressive tone either. Instead his face broke into a wistful smile. His eyes took on a faraway look.

"When I was with the gorillas," he suddenly announced, "I felt protected, as if nothing could hurt me."

Meriel stared at Max, astonished. She didn't know if he was talking to her, or to himself. But she knew exactly what he meant – that feeling of belonging, of being defended. She'd felt that herself when she was with her wild dog family.

She pictured herself in the wild dogs' den,

sleeping tangled up with the other puppies. She saw again her wild dog "mother," who'd raised her with her own puppies, and who'd fought so ferociously for her, when the Prof had rescued her.

Meriel didn't know how to speak about these emotions. She almost fled back up to the museum's roof. But, to her own surprise, she resisted that. Instead she stopped pacing and sat down at the table alongside Max.

"Want to come to my room?" she asked him. "And meet Travis, my weasel? He's probably back from hunting by now."

"I'd like that," admitted Max, somehow aware that meeting Travis was a great honor. "But the Prof said to stay here."

Meriel didn't often smile – she didn't have much of a sense of humor. But she did now. "This isn't school," she told Max, with a subversive grin. "You don't have to obey the rules."

Down in the basement storerooms of the Natural History Museum, the Prof had a sudden attack of sneezing. He was hunting feverishly through the oldest and dustiest specimens in the museum's collection. They were in a cabinet, tucked away at the back of the basement, a place he'd forgotten about until tonight.

He was searching for that fossil. The one Evan, the boatman's big brother, had said he'd found in caves under the Wastelands.

He was hoping his growing suspicions were wrong – that the fossil didn't exist or was a fake. But then he found it, between a stuffed dodo and a cloudy jar that contained a pickled baby shark.

It was in a cardboard box. The handwritten label was yellow with age. *Fossil crab, found in caves under the Wastelands*, it said.

His hands trembling slightly, the Prof lifted out the slab of gray rock. A fossilized creature was pressed into it, in a tangle of crushed and broken legs. The Prof examined it carefully, peering at it through a magnifying glass. There'd been a lot of damage. But he was convinced it wasn't a fake.

"So you weren't lying, were you, Evan?" muttered the Prof to himself.

He peered at it again. He could see why, sixty years ago, the museum people had thought it was a primitive crab. The legs that weren't missing ended in claws. What else could it have been?

But, since then, scientists had discovered a lot more about dinosaurs and the creatures who shared the earth with them.

Suddenly, the Prof's hands began shaking so badly he almost dropped the fossil. His worst fears were confirmed.

"It's not a crab," he whispered to himself, in an awed voice. "It's a Jurassic spider. I'm almost certain."

When the Prof went limping back to the kitchen with the fossil, Max and Meriel weren't there. He swore under his breath. It was typical of Meriel not to stay put. But where was Max? It didn't occur to him that Max was with Meriel. Apart from when she went on missions with Ellis, Meriel was a loner who lived in a secret, mysterious world of her own. Even the Prof had difficulty reaching her.

But then Meriel walked right in, with Max. The Prof had no time to be surprised or ask questions. He got straight down to business.

"Look, I know this sounds like a ridiculous theory," he told Max. "And I might be completely wrong. But I'm worried your dad wasn't hallucinating. It's just possible that spider he saw could be real."

Meriel stood in a corner. At the Prof's words, her body stiffened. Feeling her sudden tension, Travis poked his head out of her pocket. His smooth, snakelike head writhed around. His tiny black eyes glittered, looking for danger.

Max had been staring at the Prof, speechless. Finally he found some words. "Pardon me, Professor," he stuttered. "But I don't understand."

The Prof showed Max the fossil. "There's good reason to believe this came from caves under the Wastelands. I think it's a primitive spider, from Jurassic times. See its claws? Now, obviously, spiders like this are supposed to be extinct. But what if, somehow, they survived in those caves? What if one found its way up into the dome and what if...?"

The Prof stopped in mid-sentence and shook his head. He found it hard to believe his theory himself. Even as he explained it, it sounded unscientific, wildly speculative. There were far too many "what ifs" for a start.

Meriel certainly didn't rate it. She gave one of her

scornful snorts, *"Huh!* All this fuss about stupid spiders! Who's scared of them?"

For once, worry and uncertainty made the Prof lose patience. "Look, Meriel, these aren't like modern spiders. The kind you can stomp on, or flush down the drain! They're big for a start – I suspect this fossil one is just a baby."

"So my dad *could be* in real trouble?" Max said.

"He and Ellis both could be – *if* a spider like this were loose in the dome," answered the Prof, more calmly. "But, of course, I could be making a big fuss over nothing. I expect they're perfectly fine. All the same," the Prof decided, "I think I'll go out there and take a look. See what Ellis is up to."

"I'm coming too," said Max.

"I don't think that's a good idea," said the Prof.

"He's my dad," said Max, his face squinting up fiercely. "You've got no right to stop me."

"All right," said the Prof, reluctantly. And after all, he told himself, all this stuff about Jurassic spiders was probably pure fantasy.

"You coming too, Meriel?" he asked. "Help me find Ellis?" He deliberately didn't mention Jack.

He knew Meriel couldn't care less about him.

Meriel stood there, squirming. She badly wanted to say, "Course I'm coming." She felt a fierce protective instinct toward Ellis. She'd risk her life for him. Fight to the death whatever threatened him.

If only spiders weren't involved. Meriel snarled at her own fear. As if to punish herself, she dug her fingernails so deep into her palms she drew blood. She hated being so helpless. She wasn't used to it.

Suddenly, she dashed out of the kitchen, with Travis, rippling like a red flame, at her heels. She was going back up to the roof.

The Prof sighed. He knew something was troubling his ward. But he had no time to deal with it now. It would have to wait until he came back from the Wastelands.

Max said, "Isn't Meriel coming with us?" He seemed disappointed.

"Doesn't look like it," said the Prof. "She probably thinks it's a waste of her time. That we're going on a wild goose chase. And she's probably right."

"I think we should go anyway," said Max.

"So do I," agreed the Prof. "We'll drive to the

edge of the Wastelands. Then we're going to borrow a boat."

As the Prof drove them, too fast, through the streets of the sleeping city, he thought of all the new research about Jurassic spiders. Much of it was guesswork. And it wasn't widely known, because everyone was more interested in dinosaurs than in any other creatures from that period.

But some studies suggested that Jurassic spiders had been amazing predators. Even more alarming, they weren't solitary, like modern spiders. They hunted in packs, like wolves. Some experts thought they even bred like wolves, with one alpha female, a great queen spider, having all the babies, and the rest of the colony waiting on her.

"*Like wolves*," the Prof murmured to himself.

"Pardon? What did you say, Professor?" asked Max politely.

"Oh, just talking to myself," said the Prof, as he pressed down the accelerator pedal.

Down in the caves under the Wastelands, four giant spiders, using their front legs, were rolling a bundle over the floor. Inside the bundle was Ellis, unconscious and wrapped up in sticky threads.

They were taking him to present to their queen, as a gift.

They could have killed him instantly, with their deadly venom. But they had only paralyzed him temporarily. The spider queen liked her food to be fresh and still alive.

CHAPTER NINE

Ellis opened his eyes. Then closed them again, groggily.

"Where am I?" he tried to murmur. But his lips wouldn't work; they felt stiff. He was drooling like a baby.

His mind was a dizzy kaleidoscope of stars and hot, frantic colors. Slowly, slowly it began to stop whirling. Then, as the feeling came back into his body, his hands hurt like crazy, as if they'd been stabbed with a thousand pins. Suddenly, his eyes shot open.

He'd just remembered what had happened to him.

He'd been captured by giant spiders. Jack had been right all along.

"And I told him he was seeing things," groaned Ellis.

He struggled some more. But, although his paralysis was wearing off, he was so trussed up, only his head and fingers were free.

His lips were working again though. "Help!" he shouted. His voice echoed back to him, bouncing off rock. *"Help, help, help."*

I'm in caves, thought Ellis immediately.

So the caves under the Wastelands were real too.

He seemed to be hung up, pinned to a rocky wall. Had Jack seen them take him? Did anyone know where he was? Or had the ground closed up, trapping him down here forever? His guts clenched again in panic.

He screamed himself hoarse with hysterical

shouting. "Help! help!" But no human voice came out of the dark. He was totally alone. Exhausted, he hung limply in his bonds, almost weeping with despair.

He stayed slumped like that for a long time.

Then, slowly, he raised his head.

"What would the Prof think of you, giving up?" he asked himself sternly. "Or Meriel?"

He fought to calm himself down, get back in control. Gradually, the blood stopped roaring in his ears, his racing heart slowed a little. As he stared into the darkness around him, he felt his tracker's brain taking over, assessing his situation.

Now he could see that it wasn't pitch-black. As his eyes adjusted, he made out shapes, then individual, jagged rocks. They were lit by an eerie green glow, as if they were at the bottom of the sea.

Where's the light coming from? thought Ellis.

Then he realized. It came from slime mold – a luminous fungus that glows in the dark. It was everywhere, dripping down the cave walls like candle wax.

Once, in Africa, tracking a lion, he and Gift had been trapped in a cave by a rockfall. They could have died there. But they'd found another route out, thanks to slime mold, using it to light their way like a flashlight.

Thinking of that lucky escape gave Ellis fresh courage. There was always hope. But first he had to break free of these sticky threads.

He was about to start struggling again when he heard a shuffling noise, high above him. He stayed still and listened. There it was again, a creepy sound. He looked up, his flesh crawling. The cave was as high as a cathedral. In the roof, among the green, rippling shadows, he saw stalactites hanging like chandeliers.

Anchored to them was the most amazing web Ellis had ever seen. It stretched across most of the roof space and its guy ropes vanished into darkness.

Ellis's body tensed. Directly opposite him, a spider was shuffling slowly up the cave wall, its claws clicking on the rocks. It carried a neat package in its jaws, wrapped up in silken threads. It paid no attention at all to Ellis. Its palps were flashing on and off, sending frantic messages to something above him. It stopped, as if it was waiting.

Then, from high in the cave roof, bigger lights flashed back, just three times.

The spider on the wall started crawling upward again, faster this time.

Something shot, quick as lightning, into the center of the web and sat hunched there. It stretched out its eight legs. And Ellis saw that it was a monster spider, bigger even than the ones who'd caught him. Its body hair was reddish-brown and thick and lustrous.

Ellis gazed, appalled but fascinated. *What is it?* he asked himself.

The Prof could have told him. This was the spider queen.

While Ellis watched, the smaller spider climbed upward with its gift of food, signaling anxiously all the time. He was a male spider. Approaching his queen in any way, bringing her food, especially trying to mate with her, could be a suicide mission.

The queen peered over the edge of the web, one long, hairy leg dangling. Her eyes were like huge opals, shot through with green and orange. She had very poor sight. But she knew the male spider was approaching. She could sense his every movement, smell the giant millipede he'd caught her, and make out the luminous tips of his palps, which waved around like glow sticks.

Please don't kill me, they signaled. *Please don't kill me.*

He was on the queen's web now. He sidled up to her very carefully, offering his gift. She crouched in her web, a great hulking creature. At first she made no movement. Encouraged, the spider crept closer with his gift, one leg at a time, palps flashing manically.

Then suddenly the web shivered. In a blaze of chestnut fur, the queen reared up. Her claws scraped the cave roof, her fangs glinted. As she loomed over him, the smaller spider didn't try to run. He seemed hypnotized, or perhaps just accepted his fate. The queen pounced like a panther. With one vicious stab, she injected him with a lethal dose of venom. He convulsed instantly into a tangle of curled legs.

Ellis watched, white-faced with shock, as the queen crouched over her victim and sucked the juices out of his body. When she'd finished, he was just a dried-up withered husk. She didn't want him cluttering up her web, so with one clawed leg, she tossed him over the side. She glued the millipede he'd brought her onto her web. She could snack on that later.

Then she crawled back into the cave roof, out of sight.

Ellis saw the empty shell of the spider, light as a skeleton leaf, drifting down from her web.

It could be me next, he realized.

Desperately, but very quietly, he tried again to loosen his bonds.

CHAPTER TEN

Professor Talltrees limped up to Mars Base One with Max – still in his striped pajamas – marching like a soldier on parade behind him.

The city lights that made the night sky so bright were gradually going out. Soon, dawn would break. The first hints of pink showed in the east, over the trash mountains.

Suddenly Max let his body drop into a gorilla

slouch. He'd just remembered he'd run away from school – that there was no one here to yell at him, "Boy, stand up straight!"

They'd left the Prof's car by the *NO ENTRY* signs, then borrowed the boatman's boat from where he left it moored in a little creek.

"He won't mind," said the Prof. After all, the boatman had a personal interest in finding out the truth about those caves under the Wastelands. The Prof tried not to think about that. If his guesses turned out to be right, he feared poor Evan might have met a very sticky end.

The steel door to the dome stood open. *That's a relief*, thought the Prof. He'd been wondering how they'd get inside. But it was worrying too. The dome was supposed to be sealed tight, shut off from the outside world. The wide-open door showed something had gone badly wrong.

He and Max went inside. The Prof wasn't sure whether to close the door or not. In the end he left it slightly ajar – they might have to make a quick getaway.

Only a feeble, gray light filtered in through the cloudy glass. It was like walking into a twilight world.

"Ellis! Jack!" the Prof yelled, as he led the way into the rainforest. "Where are you?"

It was eerily silent and still. Not even a parrot squawked. No butterflies swooped by. They passed one of Jack's dangling rope ladders. The Prof stopped and stared up, as if he expected Ellis or Jack to be clinging to it.

"Oh no," he murmured.

"Oo-oo-oo," breathed Max, who was gazing upward too, and couldn't prevent a soft hoot of wonder from escaping him.

There was no sign of Jack, or Ellis. But huge webs filled the roof space. They were everywhere, anchored to the girders, slung across the rainforest trees. They were intricate and strangely beautiful, like great lacy trampolines. Water drops trembled in them like jewels.

But there were other things trapped in them too. The Prof strained to see in the dim light. There were sinister silk-wrapped bundles in most of the webs. A wing poked out from one like a scarlet fan – a macaw, or what was left of it.

"They're here," said the Prof. It was even worse than he'd feared. "They've taken over Mars Base One."

"Where are they though?" asked Max, in an awed voice. "I can't see any spiders." As he watched, a sliver of dawn light found its way through the misty dome glass. It stained one web soft pink, while the droplets in it shone like rubies.

"They're probably hiding," said the Prof. "Waiting, at the end of their trip lines." It was true, what those studies had said. Jurassic spiders must be fearsome hunters. It was like a graveyard up there, with all those withered, sucked-dry corpses. Were there any rainforest creatures left alive?

"Careful where you step!" warned the Prof.

Max had been reaching for a twig, with his grippy toes. His gorilla friends had taught him that peeling bark is very soothing in times of stress. But now he saw a thin, silvery thread attached to the twig, leading up into the trees. Max snatched his foot back.

"They've booby-trapped the place," murmured the Prof. "Look out – nowhere is safe.

"Ellis! Jack!" he called out more urgently, as they picked their way through the rainforest as if it were a minefield. Max was a large kid. He seemed so slow and clumsy, but the Prof couldn't help noting how lightly he stepped, how agile he was at avoiding the trip lines. The Prof cursed his lame left leg. For him, it was much more difficult.

"Ellis! It's me!" When, again, no answer came back, the Prof felt a sick, fluttering feeling in the pit of his stomach.

"Where's my dad?" asked Max.

"I don't know," said the Prof. Perhaps Jack had escaped and left the door open. But the Prof guessed that Jack would never abandon his dome, not while he was still alive. He hoped, at least, that Ellis had had the sense to get out.

"My dad'll be okay," said Max confidently. "I've seen his TV programs. Everything always turns out all right in the end." He tiptoed on through the forest.

The Prof was about to follow, searching for tripwires before he took his next step, when suddenly a dreadful thought struck him. *The door to the dome!* he thought. *I shouldn't have left it open!* He hadn't seen any Jurassic spiders yet. But he was pretty sure that letting them out into the big, wide world wasn't a good idea.

He'd already turned to go back and close the

door when Max's voice came drifting through the dense greenery: "Pardon me, Prof. Talltrees. But I think I've found one of those spiders."

The Prof whirled back around. "What? Where are you?"

"I'm looking through a glass wall!" called Max. "I can see a beach, some water. The spider is in the… Wait a minute!" Max interrupted himself. "There's a glass door."

"Don't go through that door!" yelled the Prof. Didn't Max realize the danger he was in?

The Prof went crashing through the rainforest, as fast as his lame leg would allow. He forgot completely about checking for trip lines.

But when he reached the glass door that led to the beach, it was shut.

"Max?" said the Prof, looking around hopefully, praying that Max hadn't gone through.

Then he saw Max beyond the door. He was just standing there, on the beach, gazing into the mini-ocean. The Prof hurried through the door to join him. "Where's the spider?" he snapped, staring wildly around.

"It's down there," replied Max, pointing into the

water. "I think it's dead," he added, in a solemn voice.

The ocean was clear as glass. Down on its sandy floor was a dark, hunched shape. It was a monster spider.

The Prof breathed a sigh of relief. "No need to be alarmed," he told Max. "It's dead." The Prof had no doubt about that – spiders can't breathe underwater. "Drowned, obviously," the Prof added.

"Maybe it fell in," said Max. "From those webs in the roof." He moved closer to get a better look. "Gross, isn't it? My dad was right. It's like something out of a horror movie."

The Prof moved closer too, wading through the shallows. For a few seconds, he forgot about their perilous situation, with other spiders probably concealed overhead. His scientific curiosity had taken over.

"Amazing," he murmured. "What an incredible creature. They should have died out with the dinosaurs." He splashed in a little further, fascinated.

But what was that around it? The spider seemed to be enclosed in a massive bubble.

Instantly, alarm bells began ringing in the Prof's

brain. He was trying to remember what he'd read about spiders. How some of them can hunt underwater, by trapping air bubbles in their fur, then stroking them into one huge bubble, like a diving bell. They tie it down with spider silk so it doesn't rise to the surface. Then they lurk inside it, waiting for prey.

I wonder... thought the Prof.

But, just as he was wondering, there was a loud *whoosh*. The wave machine came on.

The ocean heaved. Its smooth surface broke into swirls and ripples.

The Prof stared down through the waves, frowning. Now he couldn't see the spider very well at all.

But what was that? *It's just a movement of the water*, the Prof assured himself.

Then it happened again. Inside its air bubble, one of the spider's legs seemed to twitch.

"Run!" yelled the Prof, as the prehistoric predator sprang out of the ocean in an explosion of spray. It landed, catlike, on the sand. Its pearly eyes stared blindly around. But its feet were sniffing, sensing ground vibrations, trying to locate its prey. There!

It leaped around. It had found them.

But by then, Max and the Prof were through the glass door. It closed behind them. As the spider scurried up on the other side, the door began to slide open again. The Prof struggled to stop it. "I can't hold it! It's opening!"

"Excuse me, Prof," said Max politely, shouldering him aside. With brute strength, Max held the door shut. But the spider didn't give up. Furious at being denied its prey, it hurled itself at the glass wall, like a battering ram.

"Watch out!" yelled the Prof. He expected the glass wall to shatter and the spider to come flying through.

But the glass wall didn't break. With a sickening squelch, the spider splattered against the inside. As its body slid down, it left a spider imprint and two streaks of venom from its fangs.

"The glass held!" said the Prof, amazed. Then he remembered how Jack had boasted that all the glass in Mars Base One was armored to repel aliens.

The trouble was, the aliens were already inside.

"Can I stop holding the door now?" asked Max.

"Yes," said the Prof. "It's really dead this time."

The Prof gazed anxiously up into the rainforest canopy. He couldn't see any more spiders. It all seemed very quiet up there. But surely there must be others? A single spider couldn't have spun that maze of webs, set all those trip lines.

Then they heard someone calling through the rainforest. "Professor Talltrees? Is that you?"

Jack Nelson came crashing through the trees, not caring whether he broke any trip lines. He was armed to the teeth, with anything he could use as a weapon – kitchen knives, metal pipes, even a broom handle.

"Dad!" cried Max. "You're safe!"

Jack stared at the shambling figure in striped pajamas. At first he hardly seemed to recognize him. Max had shot up since Jack had seen him last. He was bigger than his dad now.

Finally, Jack said, "Max, what are you doing here?"

"Never mind that now," said the Prof. "Where's Ellis?"

"Those spiders are real," said Jack. "I was right all along."

"For heaven's sake," urged the Prof. "Tell me. *Where's Ellis?*"

Up in the roof, unnoticed by any of them, there was frantic clicking, a flurry of tiny flashing lights.

"The spiders took him," said Jack, "down a trapdoor, in the desert."

The Prof struggled to control his horror. "How long ago?"

"Don't worry. I'm going to get him!" cried Jack, heroically. "Those brutes won't beat me."

The Prof snapped, "This isn't TV, Jack! This isn't one of your big adventures! This is Ellis's life! We need outside help."

"No!" Jack insisted. "We'll deal with this alone. I don't want any bad publicity for Mars Base One. We can still save the project!"

Max looked from one to the other of the shouting adults, his big face creased in dismay, his toes instinctively searching for twigs.

The Prof took deep breaths, tried to calm himself down. "Jack," he said. "It's too late for that. You don't know what you're dealing with. I've never seen anything like these spiders before. They've been evolving quietly in those caves for years under mountains of man-made garbage, and they're still thriving! They hunt with trap lines, trapdoors, underwater – their hunting skills are incredible—"

"Just let me at them!" Jack butted in.

"What, with those weapons?" said the Prof. "Be realistic! You don't stand a chance!"

"What about rat poison? There's some in my storeroom – in case rats from the trash mountains get in."

"You're not listening, Jack." The Prof frowned. "I've just told you. Rat poison won't kill these creatures—"

"Pardon me," said Max, anxiously, "but there's something up in that tree. I think—"

He had no time to finish his sentence. In a split second, a looped thread snaked down from above, dropped over Jack's head and tightened like a noose around him, pinning his arms to his chest. He dropped his weapons.

"Dad!" shouted Max, too shocked to react.

With deadly precision, more loops dropped from the roof, binding Jack even tighter. He was yanked off his feet. The Prof tried to grab him, but he was already swinging above their heads, being swiftly reeled up toward the tree canopy.

"Max!" came his faint voice, from mid-air.

At that desperate cry, Max exploded into action. "I'm coming, Dad!" he yelled.

The Prof looked on, stunned, as Max dropped to his knuckles, galloped to the nearest rope ladder and swung up it.

Meanwhile, from their web lair, two spiders came abseiling down. Like a grotesque goblin, one squatted on Jack's back, its clawed legs clutching him. Jack cried out as its fangs sank into his shoulder. His body went limp.

The spider was about to take a second bite. But then there was mayhem.

"I'm here, Dad!" Max roared.

He came crashing through the canopy like a cannonball, in great swooping one-armed swings. As he smashed through webs and trees, with his free arm he tore off branches and pelted them at the spiders who'd snatched his dad.

"Leave my dad alone!" he howled.

Open-mouthed, the Prof watched the rescue from below. Ripped-off branches and a blizzard of leaves rained down. Web tatters floated everywhere. And all the time Max was screeching – furious ear-splitting gorilla shrieks of rage and distress.

The two spiders shrank back under the hail of missiles. They weren't used to any resistance, let alone a frenzied smash-and-grab raid like this one. For a few seconds, they left Jack unguarded, twirling at the end of their fishing lines.

Like an avenging angel, Max came shrieking through the canopy, destroying everything in his way. With a last triumphant scream, he swooped down, grabbed Jack's trussed-up body and slung it over his shoulder.

Then he started down another rope ladder, slower now because of the burden he carried. The Prof hurried through the forest to meet him.

He found Max kneeling by Jack's slumped body. The Prof could scarcely believe that this schoolboy in striped pajamas had just performed the most reckless and daring rescue he'd ever seen in his life.

"They've killed my dad!" said Max, gently unwinding the sticky threads from around Jack's body. "They've killed him!"

Then Jack's eyelids fluttered.

"He's alive!" cried Max, joyfully. "Dad! Dad! Are you okay?"

Jack groaned. He was already coming around – the spiders hadn't had time to give him a full dose of paralyzing venom.

The Prof quickly checked Jack's breathing and heartbeat. "He seems all right," he said. "He just needs time to recover."

But, up above them, the spiders were regrouping. Their driving instinct was to serve their queen. Jack was a big, juicy food offering. They were determined to get him back. Other spiders came out of their hiding places, signaling with waving palps to each other.

The Prof stared up into the roof girders, saw the winking lights.

"I think they're communicating with each other," he said grimly. These Jurassic spiders were even more formidable than he thought. They seemed to cooperate with each other, work together. No other spider species did that.

"What are they planning?" he murmured anxiously, his eyes flickering around the roof space.

Suddenly, like a crack commando force, spiders started abseiling down.

"Can you walk, Jack?" the Prof asked, urgently. Without waiting for an answer, he snapped orders at Max: "Take your dad outside. Stay with him. Shut the door. Don't let any spiders get out."

"What about you?" said Max.

"I'm going to get Ellis," said the Prof.

"No, no," protested Jack feebly, through half-paralyzed lips. "I'm not leaving my dome!"

"Come on, Dad," coaxed Max, helping him up. "You're not well. Better do what the Prof says."

The first spider landed with a soft thud nearby. It was creeping toward them. They heard its scrabbling legs and clicking claws.

"Go on!" said the Prof urgently.

Max dragged the staggering, still protesting Jack away.

As they left the rainforest, Max took a quick glance over his shoulder. But the Prof had already disappeared.

CHAPTER ELEVEN

Meriel stood by the sign saying *DANGER!* with a scowl on her face. The Wastelands stretched before her: reeds, twisty creeks, swamps, trash mountains, all pink and gray in the early morning light.

She'd passed the Prof's car, parked and empty – that meant that he and Max were in the Wastelands somewhere, that they'd probably reached Mars Base One by now.

Travis flowed down her arm and bounced off into the Wastelands. It was good hunting there. He liked baby rats best. Much better to eat than their tough old parents. Meriel looked longingly after him. Being on the roof of the Natural History Museum hadn't brought her peace, like it usually did. Even mind-reading the owl hadn't worked. She couldn't fly away from the turmoil inside her head.

Finally, she'd left the roof and forced herself down to the edge of the Wastelands. But now she couldn't seem to step past the *DANGER!* sign, something she'd done many times before without even glancing at it. But then, she hadn't known about those spiders.

She couldn't bear it, how being this scared cramped her style and stopped her from doing what she wanted – which was helping the Prof find Ellis.

"Travis isn't scared," she muttered.

Of all predators, she admired weasels the most. They were her role models. If they were cornered, they'd turn and fight wolves, even grizzly bears. "Travis would think you're pathetic," she told herself.

That hit a nerve. It didn't matter to Meriel what

people thought of her. But she cared very much about losing face in front of a weasel.

She hesitated for a few seconds longer. She took several deep breaths, as if to prepare herself. Then, with her heart racing, and her eyes glittering fiercely, she followed Travis into the Wastelands.

She crossed the swamp, springing from one floating cushion of bright green moss to another – a small, slight girl, alone in a toxic wilderness.

But she wasn't entirely alone. She had friends here. As she neared the lagoon where Big Momma had made her new den, Meriel became more cautious. She crept through the reeds. Even *she* didn't want to startle Big Momma. The gator might snap before she realized who Meriel was. One bite from those snaggle teeth could take off your arm.

But Meriel suddenly wanted to see Big Momma, to pat that scaly snout, to mind-read her, if she could. Sharing the power of that formidable armored beast, even for just a few minutes, would be bound to give her courage.

She could hear the little gators cheeping, making their shrill bird-like sound. Their mother wouldn't be far away.

"Hey, Big Momma," called Meriel softly, knowing the gator, like a pet dog, would recognize her voice. "Where are you?"

Meriel crept through the reeds, onto the lagoon shore. She didn't even see the thread of silk that she broke with her foot.

Early morning mist drifted over the water. As she peered in, she could make out the ruins of the drowned theater. And a blurred shape, huge and dark, streaking up from the depths.

"Big Momma?" said Meriel, doubtfully, already backing away.

The Jurassic spider snatched her from the bank. Quick as lightning, in a storm of spray, it clasped her in its front legs. Then it plunged back with her into the lagoon.

Meriel had no idea what had grabbed her. For a few seconds, like a cornered weasel, she fought for her life, biting and scratching in a tangle of hairy limbs. Then she opened her mouth in a silent scream. Water gurgled into her lungs. Her brain exploded into dazzling stars. Then darkness rushed in...

* * *

Meriel woke up, coughing. Violent spasms racked her body as lagoon water spewed out of her mouth. She hung, sick and dizzy in her bonds, her wet hair stuck to her face.

Then, slowly, she raised her head. She remembered being grabbed off the bank. She remembered drowning. Her mind was in chaos, whizzing in all directions, like a firework display. She couldn't figure out where she was or why she was still alive and breathing. She still didn't have a clue what had captured her.

But she realized she was tied up. For a few seconds, she struggled wildly. Her bonds didn't break.

Then she turned her head. And found herself staring straight into a human face, a few inches from her own. It was a face from a nightmare – smashed, with no nose, and white, staring discs for eyes.

Animal instinct took over. She was so frantic to get away from that face that she attacked her bonds again. In a mad frenzy she clawed at them with her sharp, talon-like nails. She felt some of them slacken. She wiggled out of the rest. But she still wasn't free! Her thrashing arms connected with something else. Frantically, her hands pressed against it. It was some kind of stretchy wall. She made her hands into fists and punched a hole through the wall. Immediately, the big bubble she'd been imprisoned in burst into a blizzard of smaller bubbles. Meriel felt herself being whisked upward, carried by the air bubbles trapped in her clothes, her hair. She looked like a glittering, silvery sea nymph rising through dark green water.

Her head broke the surface into the bright -morning light. She took in a great lungful of air.

Splashing, blinking in the sunshine, she gazed around, trying to get her bearings. Instantly, her panic lessened. There was Big Momma, basking on the bank with her babies, waiting for the sun's heat to warm her up.

"Big Momma!" yelled Meriel. She began desperately doggy-paddling that way. For her, the great armored predator meant safety.

Below her, her captor, crouched in its own separate bubble, had its leg on a trip line. The trip line was connected to its larder, the bubble where Meriel had been stored. The spider wasn't too worried when it felt tugging. Lots of its victims squirmed around. But when the line went dead, it broke free of its own bubble and swam over to investigate.

Its larder wasn't there any more. Its prey had escaped. It shot to the surface after Meriel, its legs streaming behind it.

Meriel was crawling up the bank when it surfaced like a sea monster from the deep and lassoed her leg. She screamed with rage and twisted around with her hands clawed and her teeth bared. Then she saw her pursuer, its body sleek from the water, its eight, jointed legs scrambling up the bank after her, its pearly eyes glowing like twin moons. It lassoed her other leg and began reeling her in.

Meriel didn't even have time to scream. But Big Momma had seen the spider. A growl rumbled from deep in her body. She rose up on her four legs, her jaws gaping open to show her red throat and glinting, razor-sharp teeth. Then she attacked.

Big Momma galloped past, breaking the spider's lasso lines. Meriel, freed, climbed further up the bank. The spider felt the ground shaking from Big Momma's charge and reared up. Only this time it wasn't facing puny *Homo sapiens*, but a species that, like itself, had survived since Jurassic times.

Like lightning, the spider stabbed downward. This time, though, its lethal fangs were useless. They couldn't penetrate Big Momma's scaly hide.

It tried to scuttle away. But Big Momma's crushing jaws seized its body. Its palps signaled frantically, their lit-up tips flashing for help from its fellow spiders. But no help came. It didn't know that it was the only spider, so far, to find a way out of the dome.

Big Momma dragged it into the lagoon and began the death roll that would drown it.

Meriel watched from the bank as Big Momma rolled over and over. In the cloud of spray, Meriel could see nothing but a gray thrashing tail and wildly waving spider legs. Then, suddenly, Big Momma surged up like a gray submarine. There was nothing in her jaws. Meriel got a glimpse of a floating, sprawled body. Then the dead Jurassic spider sank out of sight, back into the depths of the lagoon.

Meriel sat huddled on the bank, dripping wet, as Big Momma trotted back to her babies. So Jurassic spiders did exist, just like the Prof suspected. Meriel should have been scared stiff – they were an arachnophobe's worst nightmare. And she *was* frightened – anyone with any sense would be. But now a new feeling mingled with that fear. It was respect.

Meriel knew predators: she'd mind-read plenty of them. She knew what it felt like inside their skin. But she'd never met one like that spider, with such a sneaky, skillful way of catching its prey.

Impressive, thought Meriel, fascinated despite herself.

She'd like to know more about these Jurassic spiders. Had Big Momma killed the only one? She surprised herself by thinking, *That would be a shame*.

And then she surprised herself even more. "Wow, what if I could mind-read them?" she murmured.

It would be the most amazing, mind-blowing experience to know what it felt like to be one of those spiders. But Meriel knew that would never happen. Spiders didn't have feelings. Their brains were far too primitive and undeveloped.

Meriel was still tempted to mind-read Big Momma though. She looked over to where the big gator was nuzzling her babies, letting them slide between those savage teeth.

Meriel was curious to know something. When Big Momma attacked the spider, was she coming to Meriel's rescue? Did she have feelings for her human friend? Or was she just protecting her babies, like all mother gators instinctively do?

But in the end Meriel didn't try to get an answer to her questions.

"Best not to know," she told herself. She might only be disappointed.

Anyhow, whether she meant to or not, the gator had saved Meriel's life.

"Thanks, Big Momma," said Meriel, as she got up from the bank. Now she was more determined than ever to make sure Big Momma never went back to that zoo.

But there were other things to think about first. Mars Base One rose behind the trash mountains, glittering in the morning sun. Now that she'd met a Jurassic spider, Meriel was even more scared for the Prof and Ellis. With a look of foreboding on her face, she hurried toward the dome.

CHAPTER TWELVE

Max was sitting outside Mars Base One. He was slumped like a chilled-out gorilla, his eyes half-closed, his big hands, with their scarred knuckles, resting on his knees.

Every so often, he gave little gorilla grunts of pleasure. Which was strange, considering he'd just escaped from a dome that had been invaded by Jurassic spiders and that his dad was lying, unconscious again, beside him.

But Max had every confidence that the Prof would deal with the spider problem. And he knew, because the Prof had told him so, that his dad would soon make a complete recovery.

But there was another reason for Max's contentment. Before he'd passed out, Jack had told his son something. He'd grasped Max's sleeve and mumbled urgently, "Max, are you listening? This is important."

"Yes, Dad, I'm listening," Max had said.

"I want you to know something," Jack had told him, in a slurred, groggy voice. "I don't deserve you. You're a wonderful son. The best son a dad ever had."

The best son a dad ever had – those words sparkled again in Max's mind. Like precious jewels you keep taking out and looking at. Max was surprised a few words could make such a difference. He'd often felt fed up with his dad before, and deeply hurt by those years of neglect. But, for the moment, those painful feelings had melted away.

Instead, he felt strangely peaceful and happy, sitting here in the Wastelands, with the sun warming his face, guarding Jack. It was the longest time he'd spent with his dad for years. And the longest time ever that it had just been the two of them alone together.

Suddenly someone came darting out of the reeds.

Max jumped up guiltily, stood straight as a soldier on parade. But, as soon as he saw it was Meriel, he let his body relax again into its gorilla slouch. He knew he didn't have to pretend with her. "You're soaking wet," he said.

Meriel shrugged as if it was no big deal. She went over and tugged at the great steel door of the dome. "It won't open!" she raged. "Stupid door!" She gave it a furious kick and winced as she stubbed her toes. "Is the Prof in there?"

"Yes," answered Max. "He's in there looking for Ellis. He told me to stay outside, with my dad. Make sure no spiders got out. There's a bunch of spiders in there," Max added. "They're real. My dad didn't imagine them."

"I know," said Meriel. She kicked at the door again.

"You need the code to get in," explained Max, in his slow, deliberate way. "My dad knows it."

Meriel had ignored Jack Nelson so far, as if he wasn't in the least important to her. But now she rushed over and began shaking him.

"W-w-what?" groaned Jack.

"Give me the code to get into the dome," demanded Meriel.

Jack's eyelids fluttered and closed.

"Don't go back to sleep!" said Meriel, giving him another shake. "Give me the code to the dome. The code!"

After some more shaking, Jack mumbled a number, then his eyes closed again. Meriel let his head fall, quite roughly, back onto the grass.

"Watch my dad's head," said Max.

Meriel stared at Max, as if it had suddenly struck her that Max might care about Jack, even if she didn't.

"I'll come with you into the dome," Max offered.

"No," Meriel surprised him by saying, "you should stay here, like the Prof said. Make sure no spiders get out. And take care of your dad. He needs you."

Max nodded gratefully. "Okay, I will. Thanks."

Meriel squirmed, as if she was embarrassed by the human understanding and kindness she'd just revealed. "I'm going then," she said, brusquely.

"Be careful," said Max. "Those spiders, they're terrible." He searched for a better word. "They're... they're awesome."

"You don't have to tell me," said Meriel. "I've already met one."

"Met one?" said Max, his eyes anxiously scanning the reedy swamps and trash mountains. "What, in the Wastelands?"

"Don't worry," said Meriel. "It's dead."

"Think there are any more out here?"

"Didn't see any," said Meriel. "Besides, if there were, Big Momma would kill them."

"Who's Big Momma?" asked Max, his face creased up in confusion.

Meriel didn't explain. Instead she just said, "See you later." She punched in the code number, went into the dome, and closed the door behind her.

Max made his dad more comfortable, like an anxious parent settling a sleeping baby. Then he sat, hunched up, staring at the dome.

He'd been a lonely boy. But now he realized it wasn't only his dad he cared about. It was his new friends too: the Prof and Meriel. Even Ellis mattered, whom he'd never met.

I should have gone with Meriel, he thought.

But he knew he couldn't leave his dad out here, undefended.

His eyes went from his dad to the dome and back to his dad again.

Then his grippy toes groped for a twig and began peeling the bark off, one strip after another...

Inside the twilight world of Mars Base One, everything looked gray and blurred. Meriel waited until her eyes readjusted. Then she slipped, very quietly, into the rainforest.

Crouching under a tree, she stared up into the canopy. She saw a sea of webs up there, filling the roof space, choking the rainforest trees. They were stuffed with mummified bundles. The spiders had been feeding well.

Her foot brushed a trip line. She didn't even notice. She was too intrigued by those flashing lights.

There was a soft thump nearby. Meriel whirled around. But the spider was already leaping, clawed legs out to grab her, fangs dripping poison. Suddenly, in mid-air, a dazzling light struck the creature. It dropped to the ground and scuttled into the shadows. Meriel was blinded too. She couldn't see a thing until the light was switched off.

"Prof!" she cried.

"Meriel," the Prof greeted her. He didn't ask why she'd decided to come after all or why she was soaking wet. He just said, "Glad to see you. I could use your help." He held up a flashlight. "I found this in the storeroom," he said. "It's got a really powerful beam. Their weak eyes can't stand it."

He switched the flashlight on again and waved it around above them, in case other spiders were abseiling down. "Come on," he said. "They took Ellis down a trapdoor in the desert."

He knew the flashlight wouldn't work for long. It was a feeble weapon against the diverse hunting skills of these great Jurassic predators. Besides, he had no idea how long the batteries would last.

The Prof limped ahead, leading Meriel through the rainforest, aiming his flashlight beam wherever he saw movement, or heard a rustle.

"Look around for a trapdoor," he said, as they crossed into the desert. "It'll be well camouflaged."

The Prof was steeling himself for the worst –

Ellis might be already dead. But he still had a spark of hope.

"The trapdoor's here!" said Meriel. "I can't open it!"

The Prof hobbled over to help her. Even in his frantic haste he couldn't help admiring the spiders' skills. The door, a perfect circle, was such a snug fit, and those silken hinges were a marvel of engineering.

The Prof yanked the trapdoor open. "There's a tunnel!" He flashed his flashlight around inside. "I can't see any spiders down there."

Up in the webs, there was frenzied activity – flashing lights, scuttling hairy legs. The spiders were massing, a whole army of them, ready to swarm down in hordes and overwhelm them.

"Quickly," urged the Professor. He pushed Meriel through the trapdoor, then followed. The door sprang shut behind them. Meriel was about to dash off down the tunnel. He grabbed her arm.

"Stay absolutely still," he whispered.

The spiders could easily force up the door, with their clawed legs. But spiders respond to vibrations. And the Prof was hoping that, if they didn't detect any more movement from their prey, they might abandon the hunt.

It was torture to someone like Meriel to stay still. But, like the Prof, she held her breath in the darkness, her ears straining for any sound from above.

There was nothing. The trapdoor stayed closed.

"Can we—?" began Meriel, after a while.

"*Shhh*," warned the Prof.

They didn't move for what seemed like ages to Meriel.

At last, the Prof hissed, "Let's chance it."

He switched his flashlight on, aimed it at the floor. With its beam guiding their footsteps, they crept away from the trapdoor.

"They're not following," said the Prof, when they stopped after a few feet. Meriel could hear his deep sigh of relief.

"Think they've given up?" Meriel asked him.

The Prof didn't answer that. Instead, he shone his flashlight down the sloping tunnel. "I'm guessing this leads to the caves. But I can't see any spiders."

"Maybe they've all moved up into Mars Base One," suggested Meriel.

The tunnel took an even steeper turn downward,

through the trash strata of the Wastelands. Garbage studded the mud and rubble walls: plastic bottles, car hubcaps, an old refrigerator.

Further down, a cartwheel protruded, a bucket and a rusty metal drum marked *Highly Inflammable*.

The Prof shone his flashlight on it. "Heaven knows what's in there," he said.

Then he shrank back with a startled gasp. His flashlight had lit up a bare, white arm sticking out from the tunnel wall.

But Meriel strode confidently up to it, twisted it free like a rotten tooth. "It's from a statue in front of that drowned theater," she said, throwing it down. "How'd it get here?"

The Prof said, as if his mind was only half on his answer: "Things get moved around when the ground shifts." He flashed his flashlight around the walls. "This tunnel isn't stable," he muttered. He was trying not to think about the tunnel that Evan had climbed down, all those years ago, that had closed up completely and left no trace.

Suddenly, there was a faint tremor, as if the Wastelands was flexing its muscles. A rock clattered out of the tunnel wall. A mini avalanche of mud followed it. The Prof and Meriel stared at each other, their eyes glowing white in the flashlight beam.

"We'd better find Ellis quickly and get out of here," said the Prof.

Neither of them spoke about the unbearable questions that were in both their minds: will we find Ellis? And, if we do, will he still be alive?

"What's that?" The Prof could see a soft gleam ahead of them. "Wait here," he said to Meriel. He went limping along the tunnel. Then he disappeared.

"Prof?" called Meriel.

His voice shouted back, "It's okay. It's safe."

Meriel dashed to join him. She came out of the tunnel into a large cave.

"Wow," she said, gazing around her.

Craggy walls, crusted with crystals and glowing slime molds soared above them. So many webs lined the roof it seemed quilted with gray silk.

"Incredible," murmured the Prof.

"Where are the spiders?" said Meriel. "Any around?" The Prof turned to stare at her – her voice sounded half-hopeful.

"Can't see any," said the Prof. That was the first thing he'd checked. He flicked his flashlight again around the empty webs. "I think you're right. They've abandoned this colony, moved up into the dome."

"What's that?" whispered Meriel. "Over there."

The Prof swung his flashlight beam.

A giant millipede, a yard long, scurried out of the shadows. It rushed past, on a hundred clicking legs.

"I wondered what the spiders fed on," murmured the Prof, "before they got into the dome."

There were probably more Jurassic insects down here – a whole eco-system that had survived for millions of years. But right now that didn't seem important. All the Prof cared about was getting his ward back, safe and well.

"Ellis!" yelled the Prof, his voice echoing around the walls. "You down here?"

"There's another cave through there," said Meriel.

As they hurried toward it, a shape came creeping out of the darkness.

"Watch out – spider!" warned Meriel, as the Prof aimed his flashlight beam straight at it.

CHAPTER THIRTEEN

The Prof gave a shout of joy and disbelief: "Ellis!"

Ellis stood, blinded by the flashlight beam. He shielded his eyes, trying to see beyond the light. "Prof?"

"Sorry," said the Prof, switching off his flashlight. "We thought you were a spider." He limped forward, as if to reassure himself that his eye wasn't playing tricks. "I can't believe it's you!"

Meriel stared at Ellis as if she was seeing a ghost. She hadn't expected to find him alive. The Jurassic spiders were the most skilled predators she'd ever encountered. She knew she'd be dead herself now, if it hadn't been for Big Momma.

"Hey, Ellis," Meriel greeted him, in her usual blunt way. "I thought the spiders had gotten you." Only her face, twisted with emotion she didn't have words for, showed she was pleased that they hadn't.

"Are you hurt, Ellis?" asked the Prof urgently.

His ward looked pale. He was covered in threads of spider silk. But he seemed unharmed. He was gabbling something.

"What?" said the Prof.

"It's dead!" said Ellis, pointing back into the cave. "That massive spider, bigger than all the rest. The one that ate the other spider. It just sort of shriveled up and died!"

"This spider," said the Prof, "did you say it was bigger than the others?"

"Yes," said Ellis. "It's a monster."

"And it killed another Jurassic spider?" asked Meriel.

"Yes," said Ellis, shuddering at the memory.

"The other spider brought food. But the monster spider killed it, in about two seconds, then sucked out its insides. It didn't stand a chance."

"Wow," said Meriel, impressed.

"The queen," murmured the Prof, in the same awed voice. "Has she laid any eggs?"

"I don't know." Ellis frowned. "I'd been stuck to the wall. I was trying to get free – and when I did, I looked up again and there she was, dead, hanging from her web."

"How did you get free?" asked Meriel curiously, thinking of her own violent struggles to break her bonds in the bubble.

"Well," Ellis confessed, "I got a little desperate. I thought I'd never escape. But then I remembered. Me and Gift were tracking once in Africa. And we saw a wasp caught in a spider's web. I said, 'That wasp's going to die.' But Gift said, 'Just watch.' So we did. And it chewed its way out with its jaws, bit through one thread after another. Until it was free."

"So you chewed through the threads too?" said Meriel. "Like the wasp?"

Ellis nodded.

"Cool," said Meriel.

"That's my boy," said the Prof. Ellis's wildlife skills, his close observation of animals, had gotten him out of many tight situations.

Ellis wiped some strands of sticky web off his teeth. "It was sort of like chewing toffee. Only it tasted foul."

"You sure that queen's dead?" Meriel asked him, feeling something like disappointment.

Ellis nodded again. "Yeah. She's all dried-up. Maybe the other spiders killed her. Maybe they sucked out *her* insides."

The Prof said, "Biologically, most unlikely. The queen is the biggest, most powerful spider in the colony. Only she lays the eggs. The others would never harm her. They're programmed to protect her, to keep her alive, at any cost."

"Anyway, there's no other spiders in there," said Ellis. "Only her."

"I'll take a quick look," said the Prof.

"Shouldn't we just get out of here?" asked Ellis.

The Prof knew Ellis was right. They weren't safe yet, not by a long way. There was that unstable tunnel to face, then the Jurassic spiders up in the dome. And what if they met some coming back down with food gifts? They couldn't know yet that their queen had died.

The Prof knew, if they came down in droves, his puny flashlight beam would be useless.

The Prof knew all this. But he still told his wards, "I'll only be two seconds. He gave the flashlight to Ellis. "Here, take this. In case any others come. Remember, shine it straight in their eyes." He couldn't pass up this chance. *Just a glimpse*, he told himself. The ordinary Jurassic spiders were formidable. So their queen must be a truly awesome creature – terrifying, like the monsters of myth and legend.

But she was dead, so there'd be no danger.

"Two seconds," he promised his wards again, limping into the cave.

Meriel counted, "One, two," then padded after him. But Ellis stayed outside. He'd just escaped from the queen's lair. No way did he want to go back, even for a quick look. Just the thought of it made him feel queasy.

Inside the cave entrance, something clinked against the Prof's boot. He looked down. It was an old, bone-handled hunting knife, the blade dark with rust. He picked it up. He had no doubt who had brought it down here.

"So you got this far, Evan," murmured the Prof.

He couldn't bear to think about how the boatman's big brother had met his end. It was too horrific.

"What's that you found?" demanded Meriel, suddenly appearing at his side.

"I thought I told you to stay put," was the Prof's only answer. He slid the hunting knife into his belt. He thought the boatman would like to have it.

But he was wasting precious time. He gazed quickly up into the roof. It was just like Ellis had said. The queen's web was there, lit with an eerie green light by the slime mold, perfect and symmetrical, the most breathtaking work of art. Her vast body dangled beneath it, right over their heads. She clearly wasn't alive. Her corpse seemed light as dried leaves. It looked like an empty shell.

Perhaps she has *been sucked dry*, thought the Prof, intrigued. But he quickly rejected that. Her corpse didn't look right. She wasn't shriveled up into a tangled ball, for a start. As the Prof puzzled, the queen's remains twirled gently above them like a grotesque mobile.

Then with a terrible shock the Prof realized. "It's not her corpse!" he shouted. "It's her exoskeleton. She's molted!"

Why hadn't he remembered his biology? Molting is how spiders grow – they do it several times a year.

"You mean she's not dead?" said Meriel.

The Prof didn't hear her. His one good eye scanned the cave roof. If he was right, the queen would be hiding now, waiting for her new skin to harden, her new fur to dry out and fluff up. Then, suddenly, he saw what Ellis had missed. There was a silky gray sack, up there in the gloom, glued to a stalactite.

"It's her egg cocoon," gasped the Prof. Inside it would be more baby Jurassic spiders. And now, in the dim green glow, it seemed like they were hatching out.

Before his appalled gaze, ripples ran over the cocoon's surface. Then it started shaking, twitching, as if it were alive. Bulges popped out all over it. Then, one after another, baby Jurassic spiders burst out, each about the size of a dandelion seed head. Frail and vulnerable, almost transparent, they clung to the outside, waiting. Their tiny palps twinkled, like Christmas tree lights.

From a crevice high up in the cave wall, twin answering beams cut through the gloom.

The Prof felt his heart almost stop. "It's her," he cried. "She's signaling to the babies!"

Outside the cave, Ellis heard the Prof shouting. Forgetting his queasiness, he went racing back in. He saw Meriel and the Prof, frozen to the spot, staring upward. His eyes followed their gaze. Horrified, Ellis saw two hairy legs squeeze out of the crack where the queen had been hiding and grope around.

"Run!" he yelled. But the Prof and Meriel kept staring, as if fascinated, unable to tear themselves away.

First there was just a bunch of legs. Then came the front half of the queen spider's body, with those fearsome fangs and glowing palps. Her opal eyes shone in the gloom with a ghostly sheen. Her chestnut fur had fiery tints. Then she dragged out her abdomen, and last two legs.

Now she was fully emerged, as big and furry as a grizzly bear. She raised herself up on her eight legs and sprang, in one great flying leap, across the web to her newly hatched babies. They scuttled off the silk cocoon and into her fur, where they burrowed in and clung on.

"Come on!" begged Ellis.

But the Prof only whispered, "What a magnificent beast."

Neither of them noticed that Meriel's eyes were glazed and faraway; that she'd gone into her mind-reading trance.

As Ellis dragged at the Prof's arm, the queen's half-blind eyes stared downward. She couldn't see the intruders, but she'd locked onto their vibrations. She knew exactly where they were.

She went for Ellis first because he was moving the most.

In a blur of clicking, scuttling limbs, she raced down the cave wall. Ellis didn't even have time to run. By the time he realized he was her target, she was looming over him, her fangs ready to stab. He fumbled with the flashlight, his hands shaking. He switched it on; it lit up her fur like flames. But before he could aim it at her eyes, she swept it out of his grip with one clawed leg. It went clattering off over the cave floor.

Then something flashed past Ellis's ear. The Prof had hurled the old hunting knife. He'd aimed for the queen's abdomen, where all spiders have their hearts. The knife plunged in, to the hilt. But spider's hearts are hard things to find and it had been a hurried throw. The knife missed the vital spot. The queen didn't falter. She forgot Ellis and spun around to face her attacker.

"Prof!" yelled Ellis.

He watched, helpless, as the queen reared up over his guardian. She dragged him nearer her with one clawed leg so she could finish him off with her fangs.

"Prof!" yelled Ellis again, half-hysterical. He stared frantically around; saw a gleam behind a rock where the flashlight had rolled. He dived for it, scrabbled around, then leaped to his feet again. He had the flashlight in his hand.

He rushed toward the queen, trying to hold the flashlight steady, aiming it at her eyes.

It's not working! he thought.

She didn't shrink back, like the other Jurassic spiders. But it did distract her. She turned those big opal eyes in the beam's direction. Just for a few moments.

It was all the Prof needed. Close enough now to the queen, he yanked the hunting knife from her body, paused for a split second trying to judge the right spot...then drove it in up to the hilt, further to the right and higher up.

For a moment, nothing happened. The queen seemed frozen in her attack stance. It looked like the Prof had missed her heart again. Her claw tightened its grip on his jacket. The Prof threw one wild, despairing glance in Ellis's direction.

"Run!" he ordered his ward.

But suddenly the queen released her grip. As the Prof staggered out of reach, spasms contorted her body. Her claws clattered, uncontrollably. Then she crashed to the ground like a great tower toppling, into a ruin of fur and curled, jerking legs.

As they stood watching, her life slowly ebbed away. The twitching grew slower, then stopped. Her jeweled eyes lost their glitter. Last of all, her signaling lights faded, then flickered once, then went out altogether.

Neither of them moved for a moment.

"Is she really dead?" said Ellis, not daring to move closer.

But the Prof went and stood by her. "Yes, she's really dead," he said, in a strange, choked voice. Grimacing, he retrieved the knife from her body. He wiped it clean and stuck it back in his belt.

"You hurt, Prof?" asked Ellis.

The Prof shook his head. "Where's Meriel?" he asked, looking around.

"She must have gone out of the cave," said Ellis distractedly. He couldn't tear his eyes away from that fallen monster.

The queen seemed shrunken now, no danger to anyone. Already her chestnut fur was losing its luster. As they felt her body cool, her spider babies crawled out of her fur and scattered in all directions.

Ellis wanted to congratulate the Prof for what he'd just done, say "Great work, Prof. You finished her!" But one look at the Prof's grieving face told him that would be the wrong thing to do.

"You sure Meriel's outside?" said the Prof, with sudden anxiety.

They both looked around.

"There she is!" said Ellis.

Meriel had been here all the time. She came stumbling like a zombie out of the shadows. Ellis was shocked to see how her face mirrored the Prof's, its expression just as sad and sorrowful.

"You all right?" he asked her.

She nodded. But her eyes seemed faraway, as if she'd hardly heard his question.

"Let's get out of this place," said the Prof. "Give me the flashlight."

With one last look at the jumble of legs and fur that had once been a spider queen, the three of them left the cave.

Behind them, the baby Jurassic spiders searched for safe hiding places. Now their mother was dead, they had no protection. They would have to fend for themselves.

Meriel, Ellis and the Prof were in the tunnel, on the way back up to Mars Base One. The Prof had the flashlight on full beam to light their way. He'd forced the queen's death to the back of his mind. He had to concentrate on getting his wards back safely.

The queen might be dead, but there were still the other giant spiders to face.

"Where are you, Meriel?" he called out. "Keep up!"

Meriel didn't reply. She was lagging behind them, lost in some world of her own. She hardly seemed to notice when the tunnel started shaking.

It was more than the usual Wastelands tremor. The floor was heaving, the walls spewing garbage. Rubble rained on them. An old copper pipe clanged down, just missing Ellis's head.

"Run, you two!" gasped the Prof, holding onto the walls for support. He knew he was slowing them down with his lame leg. "Here, take the flashlight," he said to Ellis.

"What and leave you down here in the dark? No way!" said Ellis. "No *way* are we doing that, are we, Meriel?"

Meriel was supposed to back him up. But she didn't. Instead she stared at Ellis as if she'd never seen him before.

Ellis was struggling to stand as the tremors grew wilder. It was like being on a ship in a stormy sea. The Prof couldn't hold his flashlight steady – the beam swung all over the place. There was an ominous grinding of rock against rock from deep underground. With a grating roar, a crack appeared in the tunnel floor between the Prof and his wards, and gaped like a wound.

"Watch out!" warned Ellis, leaping back.

But Meriel almost walked straight into it. Ellis saved her, just in time.

"What's the matter with you?" he yelled, shaking her. "You sleepwalking or something?"

Suddenly the dazed look left Meriel's eyes. She seemed to snap out of her trance-like state. "Come on," she said, leaping over the crack to join the Prof. Ellis followed her.

"We're not going ahead without you, Prof," insisted Ellis again.

"Course we aren't," said Meriel, taking the Prof's arm. "Who said we were?"

As the three of them struggled uphill, the tunnel hurled them around like a bucking bronco. They bounced off the walls and sprawled on all fours.

"Not far now," gasped the Prof.

Suddenly, the shaking stopped. For a few seconds there was an eerie stillness. Then they heard a distant roaring, like a monster suddenly set free. Ellis turned around and looked back down the tunnel, toward the caves. He could see a dull red glow in the distance.

"Oh no," he whispered.

It was flaring brighter, coming closer, released from deep below the Wastelands. Acrid black smoke came drifting ahead of it. Meriel began coughing.

"It's a flash fire!" yelled the Prof.

Afterward, Ellis couldn't remember how they made it back to the trapdoor. They staggered on blindly, choking in smoke, gasping for air, with the tunnel rocking and the raging fire pursuing them. If one fell, the others hauled them up. For one heart-stopping moment Ellis felt the fire scorching his back, realized there was no way they could outrun it. Then, behind them, there was a clattering roar. Ellis turned back to look. There was no red glow anymore. Instead, the Prof's flashlight lit up a wall of trash and rubble that completely blocked the tunnel.

The fire won't get past that, thought Ellis. At least they wouldn't get burned to death.

But, as Ellis gazed, horrified, red veins appeared

in the tunnel walls. The fire had found another way through. It was racing like blood through the splits and cracks toward them.

But by now they'd at last reached the trapdoor. The Prof threw it up and they dragged themselves through, retching, in their smoke-blackened clothes. As they rolled aside into the dunes, a geyser of fire suddenly shot out of the tunnel they'd been in seconds before.

Then they were up and running again. The Prof's flashlight felt hot to the touch as he flashed it around the dome roof. Now they were crashing through the rainforest. An army of spiders came abseiling down from the canopy. The air was thick with them.

"Look out!" yelled Ellis.

With a sickening lurch the ground heaved. The flashlight flew out of the Prof's hand. There was another teeth-rattling quake, that sent Ellis spinning into a tree trunk. This time, the whole dome shook. The spiders were smashed against the glass walls or got their threads tangled up and hung helpless, in knots of writhing legs. Somewhere, glass shattered. A parrot that had somehow escaped becoming spider food streaked out like a green dart into the sky.

The steel door to the dome had buckled and sprung open. When they ran through it, the light outside dazzled them. Ellis stumbled around, rubbing his stinging eyes.

Then he was aware of a figure shambling past him. It was Max. Max put his shoulder to the steel door and, using his great strength, forced it shut, so no spiders could escape.

Someone else grabbed Ellis's arm. It was Jack Nelson. "We aren't safe here," the explorer said urgently. "Get into the boat."

They piled in: the Prof, Ellis, Meriel and Max. With Jack steering they sped along the twisty creeks, away from Mars Base One.

Ellis slumped in the boat feeling dazed and battered. But already his tracker's brain was taking in details. And he noticed that Max had found Travis somewhere. The tiny ferocious red hunter was looped around his neck. Ellis had never seen Travis that trusting with anyone except Meriel.

But then Ellis forgot about Travis. Because they were at the edge of the Wastelands and Jack stopped the boat. They all looked back toward Mars

Base One. The fire, made fiercer by drums of inflammable chemicals dumped in the Wastelands, had spread through the dome. By now it was raging. The whole dome glowed crimson as the fire blazed, consuming everything inside. The rainforest trees burst into flames, like gigantic fiery flashlights. Glass panes blew out, with huge explosive bangs. For a long time, black smoke hid the scene, but when it drifted away on the breeze they saw the dome again. Now only the steel girders stood, white-hot, like the ribs of some enormous dinosaur skeleton. The reeds all around were a sea of flames.

Then, from the heart of the Wastelands, came a last, great convulsion. They could feel the shock waves from it rocking their boat. Before their astonished gaze, a huge abyss opened up under Mars Base One. The remains of the dome twisted and groaned. The metal girders ripped apart. Then Mars Base One collapsed into the chasm in a heap of mangled metal.

With a final shudder, the ground seemed to close again. The Wastelands had swallowed another big dream. Only some stumps of jagged metal sticking above ground and broken glass scattered everywhere showed that the dome had ever been there. Clouds of black smoke drifted toward the city, hiding the sun. But the fire seemed to be burning itself out.

Jack sat, stunned and silent, as the last ripples from his dome's destruction washed around their boat.

"At least all those spiders must be dead," said Ellis, to no one in particular. Even Jurassic ones couldn't survive that inferno. "Good riddance!" he added.

Meriel shot him an angry, reproachful look.

What's her problem? Ellis thought. She should be celebrating. They could have been killed by Jurassic spiders, or buried alive, or incinerated. They were lucky to be alive.

But his guardian, too, seemed strangely subdued. What was wrong with them both? Personally, Ellis thought it was a big shame about Jack's dome. But he knew the Prof and Meriel weren't grieving for that. Meriel had hated it with a passion and the Prof hadn't exactly approved.

"You all right?" Ellis asked the Prof.

The Prof didn't answer that question. He just said, "My car's over there. Let's go home."

CHAPTER FOURTEEN

A few days after the destruction of Jack's dome, Ellis and the Prof were sitting in the kitchen of their apartment in the Natural History Museum. They were talking about their escape from the caves. Meriel was with them, but her mind was obviously somewhere else. She was staring out of the window into the museum garden.

"I'm covered in bruises," said Ellis, pulling up his

sleeve and showing the Prof a spectacular blue and purple one on his arm. "And I still feel a little woozy from that venom."

"I just wish I hadn't had to kill the queen," said the Prof, pushing his breakfast toast around on his plate.

Ellis pulled down his sleeve again. He thought, *So* that's *what he's been brooding about*. He should have known. He should have remembered what Jack had told him – how the Prof had beaten himself up for killing that cobra, even though he'd done it to save Jack's life.

"You had no choice," Ellis pointed out. "She would've killed us. Besides, she'd have died anyway. The fire would've finished her, or the caves collapsing."

The Prof nodded. He knew all that. But somehow it didn't make him feel any better. The spiders were a unique species that had survived in the caves since Jurassic times. And their queen was the most magnificent creature the Prof had ever seen. But now not a trace of them was left. They'd all been incinerated and the ashes swallowed up by the Wastelands.

Ellis got up from his chair. He wasn't mourning the Jurassic spiders. As far as he was concerned, the world was much better off without them.

"Aren't you late for school?" asked his guardian.

"It's vacation," Ellis reminded him.

"Is it?" said the Prof vaguely. "So what are your plans for the day?"

"I'm going to meet Max Nelson," said Ellis. "I'm going to introduce him to some friends of mine. What are you doing?"

"Still working on those mammoth bones," said the Prof. "But I've got a meeting too, with the boatman, down in the Wastelands. I'm going to give him Evan's hunting knife."

Ellis frowned. No wonder the Prof looked extra solemn. He wasn't just grieving for the Jurassic spiders. He was thinking about what he'd have to tell the boatman – that his big brother almost certainly died down there in the caves.

"Are you going to say the spiders killed him?"

"No," said the Prof. "It's too horrific. Besides, we don't know that for sure."

"I do," said Ellis shuddering. "I bet that queen did it. I mean, how old do you think she was?"

"I don't know," the Prof said. "Some modern spiders live thirty years. I'm guessing a queen Jurassic spider could live twice that – maybe longer."

"So it was her!" said Ellis. "When you give the boatman Evan's knife, tell him you used it to avenge his brother. He'll appreciate that. Besides, that queen was evil!"

The Prof frowned. "I don't believe that," he said. "Animals can't be evil. They just do what they do – it's instinctive. And creatures like spiders don't even have proper brains. They're just hunting machines, pure and simple."

Suddenly Meriel spoke up. They'd both assumed her silence meant she was mind-reading something out in the garden, maybe a sparrowhawk or a squirrel. But she must have been listening all the time.

"I'll come with you to the Wastelands," she told the Prof.

The Prof looked surprised. Unless she was on a mission, Meriel didn't usually choose to be with people. She preferred the company of animals.

But he said, "Let's go now then. I want to get this meeting over with."

* * *

An hour later, Meriel and the Prof were at the edge of the Wastelands, waiting for the boatman to arrive.

The Wastelands looked serene in the sunlight and not at all threatening. There was a great scorched area at its center, where it had gulped down Mars Base One. But that would soon recover. Reeds would grow there again and there would be nothing to show that Jack's dome had ever existed.

Meriel was dancing around, restless as always. But she was twisting her long hair, almost savagely, around her fingers. The Prof knew that sign – it meant she wanted to tell him something important.

Finally, she came out with it.

"Remember down in those caves?" she began.

"Yes," the Prof encouraged her.

"Well, I read the queen Jurassic spider's mind," she said. "Just before she died."

"What?" said the Prof, astonished.

Meriel repeated herself impatiently. "That queen spider – I read her mind."

"Could you mind-read the other spiders?" asked the Prof.

"No," said Meriel. "They didn't have brains like ours. But she did."

The Prof shook his head in wonder. "That's incredible," he said. It was obvious that she'd been the alpha spider, much bigger and deadlier than the rest. But he'd never have guessed that her brain was superior to theirs.

That amazing discovery made her death seem even more tragic. "Such a waste," the Prof murmured.

He was hungry for more details. What was it like being a queen Jurassic spider? How had it felt? He imagined a super-alertness to movement; rapid scuttlings in the dark; quick efficient killings. What Meriel said was the last thing he expected to hear.

"She cared about her babies," Meriel told him.

"She had maternal feelings?" said the Prof, astounded. "Are you sure?"

Meriel shook herself like a wet dog. She didn't like remembering it, being inside the mind of the dying spider. Feeling her desperate struggles, despite that fatal knife wound, to survive for the sake of her spiderlings. Her death throes had only lasted a minute or so. Then everything had gone black and Meriel had been whisked back to her own body.

"She cared about her babies," insisted Meriel. "Like Big Momma. Even more than Big Momma."

"Who's Big Momma?" asked the Prof.

Meriel writhed around as if she didn't want to answer. Then she said, defiantly, "You know that gator I said we couldn't find. Well, I lied."

The Prof listened carefully as Meriel told him about Big Momma.

"You're not to tell the zoo people!" Meriel finished, fixing him with one of the wolf stares she used to intimidate humans.

The Prof didn't dare smile. His ward looked so intense, so fierce. "I won't say a word," he promised. The Wastelands was a vast wilderness. And now the dome was gone it would be like before, unvisited, forgotten by city people and press reporters. With any luck, Big Momma and her babies could live here undisturbed.

They heard an engine buzzing in the distance like an angry wasp.

"There's the boatman coming," said the Prof. He had the hunting knife in his hand. With the other, he was rubbing at the scars on his face. He wasn't looking forward to what he'd have to say.

While the Prof talked to the boatman, Meriel waited. Her quick eyes flickered this way and that. She spotted a spider, scuttling under a stone. This time she didn't feel that old primeval panic. Her fists didn't clench into knots. Instead, she kneeled down and lifted up the stone. The spider had an egg cocoon on its back. It was a tiny spider, about the size of her fingernail. But still it reared up, ready to attack her.

"Hey," said Meriel to the spider, her voice softening. "You don't need to worry about me. I'm on your side."

And she laid the stone very carefully back down.

CHAPTER FIFTEEN

Max Nelson ambled along beside Ellis. His big body was hunched in its usual slouch, his arms dangling, eyelids drooping. He seemed like a boy at ease with himself, who takes life at a slow pace, who can't see the need to rush.

But beneath those slack lids, his eyes were alert and worried, sneaking looks back and forth. His toes were imprisoned in his shoes. But they were itching to pick up stones, grab twigs to peel. Max bared his teeth and chittered nervously. Then he crammed his hand over his mouth and said, "Beg pardon."

Ellis sighed. He wondered if he was doing the right thing. He knew Max was alarmed about meeting his friends. From what he'd told Ellis over the last few days, Max hadn't had a very good experience with other kids.

To take Max's mind off the meeting, Ellis asked, "How's your dad doing?" Jack had been devastated after the loss of his dome. He couldn't afford to build another, so his big space adventure was at an end and exploring Mars a lost dream.

Max said, "Well, he moped around a little. He even told me, 'That's the end of my adventuring. It's time I grew up, stopped taking such risks.'"

"Did he?" asked Ellis. Ellis didn't know how he felt about that. It would be nice for Max to have a grown-up dad. But, on the other hand, Ellis didn't like to think of Jack settling down. That would be a shame. It would make the world a little bit less exciting.

Then Max spoke again. "But then a company called that makes TV programs. And they asked Dad, 'Do you want to go looking for yetis in the

Himalayas?' So of course Dad said yes and now he's getting ready to go."

Ellis took a sharp look at Max. "Do you mind," he asked him, "that your Dad's going off again?"

Max grinned, a little ruefully. "He's never going to be any different. He wouldn't be happy, just staying at home. It'd drive him crazy. He's promised to keep in touch this time though."

Ellis nodded. He knew as well as Max that Jack wouldn't change. But he was surprised Max was so forgiving. He didn't know about those words, *the best son a dad ever had*, that Max had stored in his mind, like shining jewels.

"So where are you living at the moment?" Ellis asked Max.

"With Mom," said Max. "And when Dad comes back I'll stay with him. And when they're both away..." Max's voice trailed into silence as if he didn't know the solution to that problem.

But Ellis did. "You'll stay with us, of course," he told Max, "at the Natural History Museum. There's lots of room."

"Can I?" said Max, in disbelief. "Did the Prof say so?"

"Yes," said Ellis firmly. "It was the Prof who suggested it. And me and Meriel think it's a great idea."

"Thanks," said Max, with a shy, grateful smile. "I'd like that. I really would."

"So that's decided then," said Ellis.

But there was something else on Max's mind. Because, suddenly, he straightened up to his full height. He clenched his great fists, revealed his hidden power.

"But I'll tell you where I'm *never* going to go!" he thundered, his eyes blazing with a wild, intense energy.

"Where?" said Ellis, startled.

"I'm *never* going back to St. Dominic's!" roared Max. "Not *ever!*"

Passers-by were staring. Some crossed the road to the other side. "Okay, okay," soothed Ellis, anxious to avoid a full gorilla tantrum. "No one's *making* you, are they?"

"No," admitted Max, immediately calming down. "No, they're not. I'm starting at your school next week."

"What, City High?" said Ellis. "Hey, that's cool."

Max was slouching again now, the wildness gone from his eyes. But he hadn't stopped fretting. "These kids we're meeting, do they go to City High?"

"Yes," said Ellis. "All of them do."

"Think they'll like me?" Max asked Ellis anxiously. He'd had hopes that Meriel might be his friend. But she didn't seem to need people much. She seemed to have lost interest in him, after that meeting on the roof.

"Course they'll like you," Ellis reassured him. "Just be yourself."

That advice didn't seem to comfort Max at all. He gazed around, with that innocent, wide-eyed stare. They were in the middle of a housing edition. At the entrance to a tower block, near a park with a children's playground, a crowd of kids was sprawled on the steps.

"There they are," said Ellis.

"Why are we meeting them here?" asked Max, his toes knotting inside his shoes. "Who are they anyway?"

"Have you heard of parkour?" asked Ellis. "Or free running?"

Max's face creased up in a puzzled frown. He shook his head.

"Well, that's what these kids do," said Ellis. "Come and meet them."

Max shambled up. He draped himself over a low wall while Ellis did the introductions. "Max here would like to try free running," he told his friends.

"Yeah?" said a boy with dark, shaggy hair, gazing doubtfully at the slumped, half-asleep figure.

"Maybe you could give Max a little demonstration," Ellis suggested.

The dark-haired boy took off, ran full tilt at some railings, grabbed them and flung his body over. He landed on a wall, ran along with hardly a wobble, then leaped for some scaffolding overhead. Monkey-like, he swung himself from one end of the scaffolding pole to the other, while everyone yelled out encouragement. He hurled himself next at a concrete pillar, hugged it and tried to climb up with both feet flat against it. But he slid, panting to the ground.

"Just can't get that right," he said, shaking his head, "however hard I practice."

Ellis glanced in Max's direction. "Show him, Max," he said.

Solemnly, Max took off his shoes. Suddenly, his face broke into a grin of pure joy. Was this what Meriel meant by finding the right people to mix with?

"Go, Max," whispered Ellis, as Max exploded into action, swarmed up the pillar, onto the rooftops and started his run.

The parkour kids gazed up open-mouthed, stunned into respectful silence.

Later, Ellis was leaning against a tree, waiting for Max, when he heard a voice in his ear: *"Pssst!"*

His head shot around. "Meriel!" He was really surprised to see her. Meriel always avoided places where other kids gathered.

"Have you come to see how Max is doing?" he asked her.

"I just thought I'd drop by," she said. "I'm not staying though." She was already twitching to be off. She had important business in an ancient, neglected graveyard.

"Just look at Max," said Ellis proudly.

But you couldn't actually see him. The parkour kids had surrounded him – he was part of a big, excited group who thought his gorilla habits were super-cool.

"Don't think he needs us," said Ellis.

Meriel shrugged, as if it wasn't her concern now Max had found where he belonged. But she still said, "Will he be okay? I mean at your school?"

"I think so," said Ellis. A parkour star would get a lot of respect at City High. "Anyway," he added, "there's loads of weird dudes at my school. Much weirder than him. I'll keep an eye on him though," Ellis promised.

Meriel stood for a moment, twisting her hair. Then suddenly she blurted out, "Want to come to a graveyard?"

"To where?"

"A graveyard," Meriel repeated, impatiently.

Ellis looked at her amazed – Meriel was always such a loner. "You want me to come with you? Is this a new mission or something?"

"No!" said Meriel. "This is my own personal business. There's this cat there." As Meriel spoke she pictured the cat in her mind. It was a scraggy, orange feral cat, with a tail like a fox, that lived in the broken tombs. "I haven't seen her for a while.

She's disappeared. I want you to track her down."

Ellis stopped leaning on the wall. "Sure," he said. "Let's go."

They walked off together, away from the crowd.

"Is she still alive?" asked Ellis. "Did you try to mind-read her?"

Meriel frowned. She'd made a feeble connection, for a few seconds. But, when she couldn't actually see an animal, mind-reading it was even more hit-and-miss than usual.

"I think she's still alive," said Meriel. "She's still in the graveyard somewhere. There were moldy old bones, I could smell them. And this tombstone where she sharpened her claws..."

"We'll find her," said Ellis reassuringly. "Don't worry."

"I'm not worrying," said Meriel, shooting him a defiant look that dared him to disagree. Then she dashed off toward the graveyard, with Ellis hurrying after her.

Down in the Wastelands, something was happening. All the adult Jurassic spiders were dead, fried in the fire, their ashes buried, like Jack's dome, deep in the trash strata. The caves where the colony had lived for so long had collapsed. But a few of the queen's newly hatched babies had escaped the fire. They had climbed upward, squeezing their fragile, transparent bodies through hairline cracks in the rocks, then found their way through layers of garbage. Most had died on the journey, but five had made it to the surface.

Now the five survivors scuttled to the top of the three-yard high reeds, where they could feel the wind. They stood on tiptoe, raised their abdomens high in the air. From each spiderling, a yard-long thread of silk came out. It waved around, until the wind caught it. One spiderling went first, whisked high into the air, like a tiny balloon on a string. She was bigger than the others. Her palps, as thin as pins, lit up and signaled, *Follow me!* The other four spiderlings obeyed. Even now, they instinctively knew she was their future queen.

The tiny airborne colony sailed over the Wastelands. The Prof was gone. But the boatman still sat on the bank of a creek, his eyes sad and faraway. In one hand he clutched an old, bone-handled hunting knife.

The spiderlings floated over the housing edition where Max and his parkour friends were laughing and joking. Then over the Natural History Museum where the Prof was back in his lab, studying mammoth bones.

Way below, in the graveyard, Ellis said, "Here she is! I've found her."

Meriel came racing up, as Ellis lifted an ancient tombstone, cracked in half and raked with cat scratches.

"Whoa!" said Ellis, shrinking back, as the feral cat slashed with her claws. She spat and yowled at him, eyes blazing, fur bristling like a porcupine.

"Let me see!" said Meriel. She ignored Ellis's cry of "Be careful!" and reached her hand down into the dark den. The cat relaxed and let her do it.

Meriel felt a moldy human thigh bone, then a fuzzy bundle. She pulled it out. "She's got babies!" she said. As the little blind creature squeaked and wiggled in her hand, its mother purred and twined herself around Meriel's legs.

"You should've told me!" Meriel scolded the cat,

while Ellis didn't even try to hide the big sloppy grin on his face.

Neither of them saw the other babies, ballooning high above them. Even ordinary spiders can travel long distances this way. But these were a much tougher species. They sailed hundreds of miles before the wind dropped. They floated down to a remote mountain range. The infant queen led them underground, deep into undiscovered caves.

It was the perfect place to start a new colony of Jurassic spiders.

Animal Investigators: Killer Spiders
FACT FILE

BIOSPHERE 2

- This was a giant sealed environment designed to show that people could survive on Mars, constructed by a group of scientists in Arizona. It contained 3,800 species of plants and animals and a million-gallon sea.
- The first two-year mission began in 1991, but oxygen dwindled, the sea became acidic, crops failed, and ants and other insects thrived.
- During the second mission, disputes broke out between the bio-nauts. Two were arrested for vandalizing the project. The mission ended prematurely in 1994.

TRAPDOOR SPIDERS (FAMILY CTENIZIDAE)

- These spiders construct burrows with a corklike trapdoor made of soil, vegetation and silk. The trapdoor is hinged on one side with more silk.
- The spider waits for its prey while holding onto the underside of the door with claws on its feet.
- It detects its prey by vibrations; when the prey comes close enough, the spider leaps out of its burrow and captures it.

DIVING BELL OR
WATER SPIDER (ARGYRONETA AQUATICA)

- The water spider lives entirely underwater by trapping a thin layer of air around its body using the hairs on its abdomen and legs.
- It maintains an air reserve in a "diving bell" constructed from silk, which it anchors to an underwater plant. It replenishes the oxygen in the bell by transporting air from the surface.
- The air supply allows the spider to remain in the bell for long periods, where it waits for its prey.

MEGARACHNE SERVINEI

- This was the name given to a fossilized creature discovered in 1980, thought to be a giant spider. It measured half a yard in length – the size of a small dog – and lived around 300 million years ago.
- Later investigation found the creature to have more in common with the modern-day crab than a spider.
- But new discoveries are being made every day...

Don't miss more thrilling adventures
from the Animal Investigators in

Keep reading for a sneak preview...

CHAPTER ONE

The boy stumbled up the snow-covered mountain. There were men chasing him with weapons: spears, axes and bows and arrows. The men were howling, "Kill him! Kill him!"

The boy was the slave of a mighty shaman. He'd just stolen something from his shaman master – his master's most feared and potent magic. And now the shaman's warriors were pursuing him to get it back.

The boy had been discovered, just as he made his escape. A warrior had bawled out, "Stop, thief!" The shaman himself had roared, "Hunt the slave down! Get back what is mine!"

It was bitter winter. The warriors chased the slave across a frozen lake, murder in their eyes. On the lower slopes of the mountain, the slave turned to fight. He was covered with the swirling blue tattoos of the tribe from which he'd been captured. Like all his tribe, he was a skilled archer. And he'd made his yew bow himself, and his arrows, flighted with goose feathers.

From behind a rock, he let an arrow fly. A warrior cried out, clutched his chest and fell. As the others took cover, the boy raced out from behind his rock. He tore the wolfskin cloak from the fallen warrior's body and snatched the ax from his hand. The slave boy had always wanted a wolfskin cloak and a fine copper ax. He slung the cloak around his shoulders.

The boy should have run then. But he didn't. Because, at the last moment, he noticed the fallen warrior had a dagger stuck into his belt, with a handle carved from mammoth tusk. The boy had always wanted one of those too.

He wasted precious seconds stooping to get it, sliding it inside his own belt. He didn't see the warrior who'd broken cover and was creeping up behind to ambush him...

Suddenly, the warrior leaped up and loosed an arrow. He yelled in triumph as it went whistling into the slave's back, through the wolfskin cloak. The slave staggered and almost fell.

The slave turned and ran, slipping on icy rocks, plunging through deeper and deeper snowdrifts, with the men shrieking behind him.

At last, he turned to listen. His heart clenched with horror. Was that howling he heard?

It's only the wind, he decided.

He couldn't hear the shrieks of the warriors now. Had they given up the chase? The slave boy kept climbing, using the copper ax blade to chip handholds, footholds in the ice. He knew there was a cave higher up where he could shelter for the night. When dawn came, he'd go on, to his tribe beyond the mountains.

Will there be bears in the cave? he wondered. In his present state, he'd be too weak to fight them.

In spite of his desperate situation, the wounded

boy gave a grim smile. Using his magic, the shaman had terrorized the whole land. No one could kill the shaman – his magic protected him. He led his warriors on nighttime raids. They burned villages and kept the people as slaves. The boy's parents had been killed trying to save him and the boy himself taken captive.

But now I've taken the shaman's magic, thought the boy. *So he has no power anymore.*

But had he lost any of the magic, during his mad scramble to get away?

He opened the leather pouch on his belt to check. It was packed with moss. Hidden inside it were the seven seeds he'd just taken. They were the shaman's secret, the source of his power. The slave boy breathed a sigh of relief. The seven seeds were still safe, undamaged. He could hardly believe such tiny things contained such potent magic, stronger by far than the magic of the wolf cloaks the shaman's warriors wore.

With clumsy, shaking fingers he poured the seeds out onto his palm. They were glossy black with a scaly coating. Each had six sharp spikes, like tiny daggers. As soon as they touched his flesh, he felt a hot tingle shoot up his arm.

We are powerful, the seeds seemed to be telling him. *And all our power could be yours.*

"Destroy the magic!" the boy urged himself. Grind the seeds to powder with rocks, so they couldn't be used again by the shaman, or anyone else, to bring terror and death. "Do it now!" he ordered himself. "You must!"

But, somehow, he just couldn't. Already, the shaman's magic was starting to corrupt him. As it could most men and boys, even the bravest and noblest.

With freezing fingers, the slave boy hid the seeds again under the moss. He tied up the pouch. Then stumbled on, through a swirling blizzard.

He felt no pain from his arrow wound. The cold had numbed his whole body, right through to his bones. His feet, in his goatskin shoes, felt like heavy rocks. It was harder and harder to drag them. Soon he forgot about reaching the cave.

He just thought, *I must lie down and sleep*.

He curled up in the snow, still holding his ax. He wrapped the wolfskin cloak tightly around him and closed his eyes. He imagined himself using the shaman's magic.

It made him mighty; no man could defeat him. He was so swift their arrows couldn't catch him, so savage they scattered before him. Terrible things had been done to him – his family had been slaughtered; he'd been made a slave. And he would do terrible things in return. He would take vengeance. People would be made to suffer, just as he had. Perhaps that would ease the bitter anger and pain he felt, deep inside.

His freezing fingers felt for the braided leather band on his wrist. He had worn it throughout all his troubles. His father had made it, from the skin of the first deer the boy had hunted and killed.

The boy snuggled deeper into the snow, his head full of violent and bloodthirsty dreams. He didn't move again. Soon, his smile was a frozen mask, his eyelashes fringes of ice crystals. The hand grasping the ax froze solid. Gradually snow covered his whole body, first a light crust, then a blanket, then a drift many feet deep.

Many times the shaman's warriors came searching for him. But they never found him, or the seven seeds he'd stolen. Without his magic, the shaman's power was broken. His warriors left him.

Finally, one day the shaman himself fled and was never seen again.

No trace of the boy was ever found. But his memory didn't die. His story was told to children around village fires – how a humble slave boy had defeated a mighty shaman by stealing his magic seeds. There were two versions of this story. One said that the boy had destroyed the shaman's seeds, for the good of all. But the other claimed that, like so many other men and boys before him, he'd been corrupted by their evil power and kept them for himself.

Both versions were passed on, down the generations.

As the years passed, the snow over the slave boy's body froze. Then a glacier flowed above his corpse, crushing it with its weight, burying it still deeper.

Centuries went by. In some remote places a few people still told stories about the slave boy and the shaman's magic seeds. But no one believed they were true anymore. They belonged to the world of fairy tales.

Five thousand years passed and still the boy's body lay undiscovered, locked in its icy tomb. Until, in the twenty-first century, the glacier started to melt…

What will happen when the slave boy's body
– along with those magic seeds – is
rediscovered and sent to the Natural History
museum, home of the Animal Investigators?
Find out in

Also available:

ANIMAL INVESTIGATORS

RED EYE

A half-crazed boy has turned up at the Animal Investigators HQ, raving about an army of gulls taking over his town, led by the malevolent Red Eye. Ellis and Meriel must find a way to stop this deadly menace from terrorizing the town's people – before the death toll starts to rise.

ANIMAL INVESTIGATORS

GHOST DOGS

Ellis is investigating rumors of a haunted forest when he stumbles across a ghostly dog pack led by a strange feral boy. The air temperature plummets to lethal levels, and Ellis suspects that the boy wields some kind of deadly supernatural power. Can the Animal Investigators stop him before lives are put in danger?

S. P. GATES worked as a teacher in Africa and then in England before becoming a full-time writer. She has since had over one hundred books published and, among other prizes, has won the Sheffield Book Award twice and been commended for the Carnegie Medal.

S. P. Gates is married with a daughter and two sons, and lives in County Durham in the UK.